Prisoner

Prince

A BOY AND HIS PARENTS IMPRISONED
DURING THE FRENCH REVOLUTION

Written By:

Olga B. Kurtz

Illustrated by: Virginia Kelley

Copyright © 2016 by Olga B. Kurtz

ISBN: 154085695X
ISBN13: 9781540856951

DEDICATION

With love to my children:
Christopher and Sara
Melissa and Hank

And my grandchildren:
Nathan
Reese
Brianna
Annabelle
Olivia

ACKNOWLEDGMENTS

Writing in one form or another has always been a part of my life, but if the thought of writing a book ever flitted into my mind, it was gone just as quickly. It was only recently that I gave serious thought to the idea, and it came about through several unrelated events.

Years ago I heard about a prince who was raised by Indians. For some unknown reason, of all the important things I did forget, that thought stayed with me. Recently something clicked into place that that prince might be Marie Antoinette's son. At that time, all I knew about Marie Antoinette was that she was queen of France during the revolution, that she was guillotined, and that she said, "Let them eat cake!" which I've since found out she didn't say. It never occurred to me that she might also be a mother.

A quick check at the library and sure enough, Marie Antoinette and her husband, King Louis XVI, had four children. One of them was Louis Charles, the Dauphin (next in line for the throne). He did become King Louis XVII for a few months and died when he was ten years old. There wasn't much more about him except that for years there was much speculation about his death… nothing about him being raised by Indians.

Anyhow, for no reason I can identify, I asked the librarian for more information about Louis XVII. A week or so later, through the wonderful Interlibrary Loan system, I had a translation of a two volume set titled, *Louis XVII, His life, His Suffering, and His Death,* written in 1855 by a Frenchman , Hyacinthe Alcide du Boise de Beauchesne. The author told a gripping, tragic story of the mistreatment of the boy who had the misfortune to be the son of Marie Antoinette and King Louis XVI during the French revolution. That did it. I was caught up in the tragedy of the royal family and the chaos of the period. It was de Beauchesne's work that inspired me to try to re-tell this compelling story.

At about the same time I discovered the Akron Manuscript Club, founded in 1929. It is the oldest writer's group in Ohio. Members meet to critique each other's work. When I tentatively brought a few pages about the prince, the group was encouraging enough that I continued writing. **Prisoner Prince** was the first of what has developed into a revolution trilogy. Next was **Crazy Spider,** published in 2006, about another unfortunate prince during the Russian revolution. and **Revolución Reporter** about the Mexican Revolution, published in 2015. The progress for these three historical novels was so casual that I almost lost sight of the happy coincidences that brought it together. I am indebted to:

- Hyacinthe de Beauchesne who researched for twenty years to collect details about the royal family's imprisonment and then wrote about them so vividly.

- The Public Library system that made such a resource available to me, and to the staff members who have always been so helpful.

- Akron Manuscript Club members who encouraged the conception and participated in the gestation of all three novels, Their suggestions and guidance were, and are, invaluable.

- My daughter, Melissa Jones, who has been my sounding board and adviser throughout. All my family have been kind enough to listen to the highs and lows of the entire process from inception to publication.

- Special thanks to fellow author, A. D. Adams, for his guidance and patience throughout the publication process.

- My sincere appreciation to all of you.

O. B. K.

Contents for Prisoner Prince

As told by Leroy Louis Charles, a fictional character. Because of his name he became interested in Louis Charles, the Last Dauphin of France who was the prisoner prince.

As told by Axel de Fersen, friend to King Louis XVI and Marie Antoinette. He orchestrated the escape of the royal family.

As told by Elsa von Bradenberg, a fictional friend to Marie Antoinette. The Countess describes the antics of the little Prince, life at court, and the beginnings of the French Revolution.

As told by Gerard Gascon, a fictional character who was a guard for three years at the old castle where the royal family was confined. Gerard develops an affection for the Dauphin. He is disillusioned with the views and violence of some revolutionaries.

As told by Turgy, a cook who followed the royal family from their youth at Versailles to their end in The Temple. He sympathizes with the King and Queen as human beings, describes the circumstances of their executions, the mistreatment of the Prince, and the fury of the Revolution.

Leroy Louis Charles continues his narrative. His hobby became studying the impostors who claimed to be the Last Dauphin of France. He tells about two of the best known, Jean Marie Hervagault and the American botanist, John James Audubon. He also reports about recent DNA tests performed on the preserved heart of the little prince.

Prologue

From "Veev" to Prisoner Prince
As told by Leroy Louis Charles, a fictional character of the present.

When I was a boy, I didn't like my name at all. Now the name is on the door, right under GENEALOGY DETECTIVES, INC. I'm Leroy Louis Charles, President. I started the company, and it's doing pretty well if I do say so. I never intended to write a book, but I did. Sometimes insignificant things that seem unimportant at the time, can influence your life. This is how it all came about.

Sometimes I get asked how I got interested in genealogy. I usually answer, "Because of my name. *Le Roi* in French means 'the king.' Louis and Charles are both names of kings. I wanted to find out if I descended from royalty and could claim the throne of France."

That usually gets a chuckle or two, and I leave it at that. But there's more that I don't tell. I got my name not because there's royalty in my blood, but because of an impostor. I found out about him from my father after a silly incident at school. I was about nine or ten years old and taking French classes on Saturday morning. One particular Saturday, the teacher was telling us about the French Revolution. The revolutionaries won and did their best to kill royalty and nobles. She said that even when monarchists stood in front of the guillotine to be executed, to show support for the king, they would shout in defiance, "*Vive Le Roi!*"

Of course some smart mouth said "Veev Leroy," pointed at me and everyone laughed. All I wanted to do was hide under the desk. It didn't matter one bit that the words meant "Long live the king!"

I came home storming, faced my Dad, and demanded to know why he gave me a dumb name like Leroy. My Dad calmed me down enough to find out what happened at school. Then he told me it was time I learned a little family history. I plopped down scowling and reluctant, but knew I better listen.

According to my Father, some of our ancestors came to America during the French Revolution. They settled in Greenwich, New York where there was a community of other Frenchmen. Living among them was a man who called himself Mr. Leroy.

"You know now that *le roi* means 'the king'?" I nodded, still sulking. "Well his name was suitable because Mr. Leroy claimed to be the *Dauphin*. In France that's the title for the male heir who's next in line for the throne. Mr Leroy's story was that his parents were Louis XVI and Marie Antoinette. After they were executed, he was able to escape from prison because another boy was substituted in his place. He came to America and lived the remainder of his life in Greenwich as Mr.Leroy, the rightful king of France,"

In spite of myself, I blurted, "You mean he really thought he was a king?"

"Yep, he sure did. He claimed to be Louis XVII whose actual name was Louis Charles." He poked me in a kidding way and said, " Charles, I will remind you, is our family name."

At no response from me, he said, "I will continue. You should know that in Greenwich, Mr. Leroy was pretty much accepted even though he was often a topic of conversation. One evening one of our uncles or cousins, whose name happened to be Louis Charles, was skeptical of Mr. Leroy's claim. 'If Mr. Leroy can be Louis XVII, we should name a boy to be *Le roi* Louis Charles. That would put a king right in our own family. Our claim is just as good as his.' When his son was born, that's just what he did."

My Dad looked at me as if waiting for my reaction, but right then, I wasn't sure what to think.

"That my son is how the first one got his name. Eventually the *Le Roi* became Leroy. You could say we have our own dynasty." He stood at exaggerated attention, saluted me, and proclaimed, "Veev Leroy!"

Can you believe it? My own father!

It stuck. Friends and family to this day call me Veev. But for me that was only the beginning. I took it from there. I couldn't help wondering. Mr. Leroy was an oddball, but what about the real prince? What happened to him?

It didn't take me long. I found him with one trip to the encyclopedia right under Louis XVII. There wasn't much information. Louis Charles was known as the Last Dauphin. He was declared to be king for a few months, but he didn't know it because he was in prison. He was ten years old. That did it. I was ten years old. I thought of myself behind bars. All alone. Scared. Who put the prince there? Why? Was it a dungeon like in the movies? Was he tortured? I didn't think about him all the time, but I couldn't forget about him either.

Louis Charles got to be a part of my life. I called him Charlie. The frustrating part was that the library had shelves of books about the French Revolution and about his parents, but precious little about their son. There was more about his older sister, Teresa, than about Charlie. What with me picking up information on my own and history at school, without even realizing it, I got interested in history. It was my major in college.

I think it was in my junior year. The grade for the whole semester in one of the classes depended on one term paper. Right after I got the assignment, Charlie popped into my mind. Maybe I could do the paper and find out more about him at the same time.

For once I didn't wait till the last week.

The librarian at our local branch always listened and tried to help. She came through again. Very soon I got a two-volume set with the title, **Louis XVII, His Life, His Suffering, and His Death** by Hyacinth Alcide du Boise de Beauchesne (talk about a name!). The title sounded like what I needed, but when I glanced through both books, I sure didn't like what I saw: small print, lots of footnotes, and sentences that were a half page long. It was more than I needed…or wanted.

I'd like to think that I was being sensible, but more likely it was Charlie prodding me again. "You wanted information. You have it. At least read a few pages." Reluctantly I did, and that's how I found out the author spent twenty years in research and was able to interview some of the people still alive who knew either Charlie or people who guarded him. I was hooked.

Those long, long sentences were not an easy read, but I got through them, and they paid off. They gave vivid descriptions of the upheaval and chaos of the Revolution. There were wrenching examples of the horrors and stupid things that can happen under conditions like that. There were lots of villains and a few heroes, and I got a different picture of King Louis and Marie Antoinette. Up till now they were portraits in elaborate robes, gowns, and wigs who didn't know much about the life of ordinary people. De Beauchesne portrayed them with the same feelings, strengths and weaknesses as the rest of us.

The best part was that the author was true to his title. Everything helped to explain what happened to poor Charlie. As a small child he lived in the luxurious palace of Versailles. He was a handsome boy, smart, likable, a golden prince. The problem was that he had the misfortune to be the son of King Louis and Marie Antoinette when hatred was growing against the monarchy. After both parents were guillotined, Charlie's circumstances changed drastically. Even in those cruel times, no adult should be treated as he was, never mind a child who was completely alone and defenseless.

Stories started circulating that he escaped or had died. An autopsy was done on a body. It was such a sloppy job that the report didn't even mention Charlie's deformed ear or his vaccination scar, and illnesses he did have were misdiagnosed. The confusion and uncertainty made it easy for imposters to appear. Mr. Leroy wasn't the only one. There were many others. De Beauchesne called them 'pretenders.' These pretenders eventually took me in another direction. Little by little I started collecting their histories. They were one bunch of pathetic, bizarre, and funny characters. Tracking them down developed into a hobby that took lots of research and detective work. It just so happens that these are the same skills needed in tracing genealogies. And that's how my business, Genealogy Detectives, got started.

There you have it. A thriving business, an absorbing hobby, and a silly nickname, all because I was given the same name as a little boy who lived over two hundred years ago. But I must say, after spending most of my life in Charlie's company, I'm proud to carry the name. It's dignified and honorable.

I have two children as different from each other as they can be. My son is Leroy Louis Charles, Jr. He understands why he was given the name and knows enough about poor Charlie's life that he feels as I do.

My daughter Melissa is very much like her mother, pretty and smart. Since she was a little girl, it has been her habit to pop into my office with or without a reason. One of her visits was a turning point. I'll have to explain how this came about.

My life was involved with Charlie's history because of my name. I sure didn't think anyone else was interested. I found out different by sheer accident. I was driving alone and tuned to NPR (National Public Radio). I was only half listening when I heard Louis XVII mentioned. Scientists in Holland and Germany were doing DNA tests on what was believed to be the actual heart of the Dauphin.

<u>A heart preserved for 200 years</u>

Holy mackerel! They were talking about Charlie's heart! My mind starting racing. How could somebody have gotten the heart? Where did they get it? Did they steal it? Why would anyone do such a thing? How was it preserved for two centuries? Why would scientists in two countries give a darn whether it was or wasn't Charlie's heart? I probably made a pest of myself by bringing the subject up in conversations with family, friends, and clients at every chance I had, but I was glad I did. The result was that they passed on to me newspaper and magazine articles about the tests that I could have missed. These articles supported information I already knew. They were spread over my desk when Melissa dropped in.

My office is filled with all the articles, files, charts, and books that I collect and that I need in my work. It was Melissa's habit to try to bring some semblance of order to the accumulation. Sad to say, the next time she came in, it was just as bad. That gave us opportunity for needling back and forth. Our usual banter went something like this.

"Dad, I don't see how you can work. It's such a mess!" She gathered the articles on my desk and flipped through them. "Here's the new stuff about the Dauphin's heart. What should I do with it?"

"Just stack it and put it on a shelf where I can get to it. I'm still reading it. I'll file it one of these days."

"Ha! That's what you've been telling me since I was a kid."

"Sugar, you're still my kid even if you did graduate from college"

She gave me one of her wonderful smiles, perched on the edge of the desk, and said, "I'm not talking just about organizing and filing, though this office sure could use it. I'm talking about doing something important."

"Like what I'm doing isn't important?" I leaned back in my chair and folded my arms. "OK smartie. How about coming up with one or two ideas that you think are more important."

She got thoughtful. I could see she was serious. "Well, you do have some really good references. Come to think of it, you probably know as much as anyone about Louis XVII and his impostors, too." This was high praise from my daughter, and rare too. But the real surprise was when she said, "Why don't you write a book about them?"

That brought me to a full stop. I just looked at her for a long moment. "Oh, come on honey, be real. Who would be interested in a kid who lived a long time ago, and didn't do much of anything except die in prison? Maybe the Charles family, but I'll bet not even many of them."

"What about these articles?" She thrust the stack in my direction. "Somebody's interested."

I answered doubtfully, "Yeah, but a book…That's a big deal."

Like it would be nothing at all, she said, "You already know all the stories. All you have to do is write them so people would want to read them." With that, she did put the stack on the shelf and said,

"Think about it, Dad." She grinned, twiddled her fingers at me, and left.

Just that casually, the seed was planted.

***

It took a long time for the seed to sprout, but it didn't die either. You might say it was there germinating in the dark. I kept mulling things. Eventually some ideas became clearer. No doubt about it, I cared about Charlie. I wanted more people to know about him. What happened to him shouldn't happen to any kid, prince or urchin.

I looked up my old term paper. The facts were there, but it wasn't exactly what anyone would choose to read. What it did do was remind me of some of the real historical characters. They were as varied, nasty, and colorful as in any Charles Dickens novels. There was Turgy, a cook who followed the royal family wherever they were put. There was Madame de Lamballe, a friend to the Queen. She was hated so much by the people that after she was killed, her body was torn apart by the mob. There was the Swedish count, a visitor to France who tried to help the family escape from Tuileries and failed. There was General LaFayette, a Frenchman who was a hero to Americans during our Revolution, but was far less successful in his own country. All of them and others kept churning in my head. Could any of these characters be used to give their own versions of what happened? And of course I wanted to include something about the pretenders. They were just too colorful to leave out.

Something else got clearer. As the Revolution got worse, so did treatment of the family. They were moved from the luxury of Versailles, to deteriorating Tuileries, and to The Tower that was finally their prison. The frame was taking shape. I started experimenting with a few pages of writing.

I don't know why I started with the Swedish count except that if the escape he planned had succeeded, it would have been a different history. I tried to imagine how he must have felt after the escape failed. That was a major snag right there. The problem was that he was the only one who could tell about his feelings. If I let him talk the way they did back then, it would be hard to read (like de Beauchesne). Besides, I probably couldn't write in that old style anyhow. On the other hand, he couldn't talk modern either. I tried for a middle way...and tried...and tried.

Nobody saw what I wrote for a long time. One day out of the blue, my wife asked, "Are you going to show me what you've been working on, or not?" The tone was more an order than a request. I was caught and might as well take the plunge. I handed her the first part told by Count Fersen. Isabel, who is a smart lady, sensed my reluctance and put my problem very neatly. "Would you rather have kindness or honesty?" She had me there. I wasn't sure which one I did want.

The upshot of it was that she did both. She made constructive suggestions, and more important, she was encouraging. I kept on writing. Eventually after many disappointments, the manuscript was accepted by a publisher. I can say without doubt, that was one happy day.

That's how it came about that right now, here in my office, on my desk close to hand, is my book, **Prisoner Prince.** On the cover in nice bold print, is my name, Leroy Louis Charles. The name looks just as good on the cover as it does on the office door...maybe better.

I would be embarrassed if anyone saw me do it, but I have a sort of private ritual. Every once in a while I pat the book fondly, salute and say, "Veev Leroy!"

#

Part I, Escape from Tuileries

June 20 - 25, 1791

Count Axel de Fersen from Sweden was friends with King Louis XVI and Marie Antoinette.
His memoir is the author's invention. The events are factual.

For much of my life I have endured a war within myself that continues to this day.

I have lived a full and accomplished life that many would say brought honor to me and to my family. My reveries should be satisfying. They are not. I am haunted by one glaring failure. It was my planning that was responsible for removing the King, his family, and their attendants from the vengeance of the revolution that was beginning in France. I try to comfort myself with the thought that mine was a small part in the course of history, but the truth remains. King Louis XVI and his wife, Marie Antoinette, were executed by the guillotine. Their children were left as orphans in prison, though it was not until many years later that I learned the true horrors of their confinement.

Hindsight of course sees errors clearly. Over and again I review the plans I made so carefully and find fault. Still in my own defense, I would hold that no human could have devised such a devious puzzle with pieces that appeared to fit and yet were wrong. Or worse, pieces that did not fit at all. It was almost as if another hand were arranging the pieces to make another picture. Always my thoughts circle to the failure, and I feel remorse and doubts. Could it have been different?

I am writing this memoir in hopes that putting ink to paper will bring some order to the jumble continuing in my mind.

I will begin at the beginning with the occurrence that changed my life.

***

Of course she was the center of attention. How could she not be? Among the dazzling exhibitions of wig and hair arrangements, one even with a bird in a cage, hers was the most elaborate. It was made up of various colors of plumes that floated high over her head and towered above all the other headdresses.

This was a masked ball, and my first social event in France. I had recently been appointed colonel to the royal regiment from Sweden as bodyguards to King Louis XVI. I had heard of the palace of Versailles and the extravagances of the French court. It was one thing to imagine such things in the mind's eye. It was altogether a wonderment to see the actual scene before me. There were countless jewels that sparkled with the lights of thousands of candles. In turn, the candles were reflected in the mirror panels lining the walls. Men and women were clad in every color of the rainbow in satins and silks and laces, every flutter of a handkerchief or a fan emphasizing each gesture. There were also uniforms equally as colorful and some downright gaudy with their gold braid, buttons and epaulettes. I also noted that trousers pulled skin tight over well-muscled legs were becoming. They were not so attractive when they revealed a plump figure, a paunch, or bowed or spindly legs.

I'm not sure whether it was simple curiosity or the audacity of the headdress, but I drew nearer to the group surrounding the lady with the plumes, and observed. Her manner was light and frivolous, even flirtatious...a furl of her fan, a girlish giggle, or a pert comment. A body moved conveniently out of my way, and there I was before her, mask facing mask. Her mouth was smiling. Her words were flippant, but her eyes did not suit her demeanor. What was it I saw? Was it boredom? Cynicism? Or could it be sadness? I was intrigued.

We exchanged the usual polite phrases, and I requested the privilege of a dance. Her reply caught me by surprise, "No, no. I have a better idea. I have need of refreshment," She tapped my hand with her fan, "and you shall fetch it. We shall have a *tete-a-tete*. If you are properly bidable, you may receive a plume as a reward."

11

Just like that. It was as if she read my thoughts.

I did bring refreshments, and we shared a bit of privacy (if such a thing were possible) on a settee at the edges of that glittering ballroom. Our conversation came easily. Neither of us was inclined to play the social games. I found I was speaking to her more honestly than to any woman before, while on her part, there was none of the posturing I noticed earlier. Was I imagining it? Her eyes seemed to lose their sadness, No, I was not wrong. There was an affinity between us.

Whatever time we spent together was too brief. Others imposed on her attention, and I was left to find my own entertainment. I did so without much enthusiasm. My mind was elsewhere until the unmasking when I made sure I was in her presence again. She glanced in my direction and fumbled slightly as she removed her mask. The group surrounding her applauded, while I stood as if rooted to the spot.

I had seen portraits of Marie Antoinette. She was always regal, imposing, dressed in sumptuous gowns and jewels, elegant and beautiful. This woman was small of stature, not at all imposing, hardly regal, and to be honest, certainly not beautiful. Yet despite these obvious differences, I was certain. The woman with whom I had felt an easy bond was the Queen of France. More important, she was married to the man I was obligated to protect.

Her eyes caught mine and held. Again I saw in them cynicism and sadness, and something else whether in the lift of her chin or in her attitude, as if to say, "Now you know. Will you be like the others?"

It was not my voice that responded, but my heart. I knelt before her. I turned her hand, touched the palm with my lips, and folded her fingers over my silent promise. I would be a true friend. When I looked at her, she was smiling, and her eyes were not sad. This woman needed me.

Soon after our meeting, I became a part of her entourage at small entertainments and dinners at the Trianon, her private smaller palace on the grounds of Versailles. To all outward appearances, this woman who was Queen, had the world to do her bidding. It did not take long to learn otherwise. At best, she was surrounded by flatterers and favor seekers. At worst, there were enemies, some obvious, and many more hidden and waiting opportunity to pounce. Within days the malevolent tongues were doing their best to spread falsehood about us. My Queen was aware of these rumors. Rather than being constrained by them, she was sometimes reckless and almost defiant in her behavior, so that I made it my business to protect her reputation as best I could. My efforts were not enough. Circumstances intervened.

King Louis XVI, father of prisoner prince.

My Queen and the King by this time had been married seven years, yet there was no heir to the throne. The King bore the brunt of criticism in this regard. The gist of the speculation and snide comments throughout the country was that the king was more interested in hunting and in his workshop than in producing an heir. This state of affairs may not have been complimentary to the King, but privately, I was not displeased.

Not long after my arrival when the rumor mill was already working at full tilt, the court learned My Queen was *enceinte*. The anticipation of an heir should have been cause for celebration. Instead it became grist for those who grasped at any means to undermine King Louis and Marie Antoinette.

A girl child was born. The King's brother, the Count de Provence, was proxy Godfather for the Spanish king. At the child's Baptism in the cathedral, the Comte took that opportunity to pounce. When the priest asked, "What name for this child?" the

Comte answered loud enough to be heard, "First we should ask, who are the parents?"

If the King's own brother in that sacred place could utter the unspeakable, I came to the conclusion that my presence was causing disruption rather than giving comfort. It was time to leave France, but not in cover of night as if in disgrace. No. I held my head high, Conveniently, the Marquis de Lafayette was enlisting an army to aid the colonies in America in their revolution to break from England. France was very willing to support any action that could weaken the strength of its rival. I took this opportunity to join the Marquis as an honest exit. At the same time, the announcement was made that I was betrothed to a Swedish heiress. Both decisions were made in hopes they would quell the ugliness.

The parting from My Queen was not easily done by her or by me. She was Queen. Her wishes were rarely thwarted. She was quite adamant that there was no reason for me to leave. I tried to persuade her that the decision was necessary for her benefit and protection. However, my most persuasive argument was when I assured her there was no Swedish heiress. When we spoke our farewells, it was with tenderness. We both knew that most likely we would not see each other again. We understood our duties. We parted as the friends we were from the beginning.

Indeed, I did not see her again for fifteen years. During that time there was more than one occasion when papas and mamas of marriageable daughters, as well as the daughters themselves, let me know that I would be a welcome suitor. On my part there were of course dalliances, but no other woman took my interest. I never married.

During my service in America, I tried to keep informed about news from France.

Although all news took weeks and sometimes months to reach us, it seemed to me that bad news always traveled faster. There was a constant stream of reports of discontent with King Louis and his government. It didn't seem to matter whether he tried to make improvements or took no action at all, he was always the villain or the goat. Criticism was also heaped on My Queen for whatever she did, but mostly for her extravagances.

Amidst the steady flow of criticism of the King and Queen and those in their circles, there was one event that brought favor to My Queen, It was the birth of another child, her first son. I could imagine her happiness. After the years of disapproval and waiting, there was an heir at last to continue the monarchy.

That bit of favor I am sorry to say, was short-lived. The next arrival of papers implicated My Queen in a scandal. It was a complicated story that came to be called "The Diamond Necklace Affair" and took months to unfold. The papers were filled with it during all that time because it had all the sensational elements of a penny-dreadful (1) novel: a Cardinal of the Church, a treacherous countess, a priceless necklace, forgeries, and (to my horror), a woman of the streets who was disguised as My Queen. That woman, in her role as Queen, was used to dupe the Cardinal and succeeded. Eventually it was proved that My Queen was not involved, but the proof came too late. That scandal added fuel to fires that were waiting to blaze.

I served in America, fought in the Battle of Yorktown, and received recognition from the great General George Washington who awarded membership to me in the prestigious Society of Cincinnati. (2) At the end of the American Revolution, I was recalled to Sweden.

It was here that I learned of the birth of My Queen's second son who was named Louis Charles. I mention his name because he and his older sister, Teresa, played a part in the drama that marked my failure. It came about like this.

It was my own King Gustav here in Sweden who made it possible for me to return not just to France, but to Versailles and so to be near My Queen again. He, as well as other monarchs in Europe, were aware and very concerned about the growing discontent against the French King. It was no secret that I shared their concern. I am a royalist. I believed then and as I do now, that monarchies are the established order and should remain so. I do not understand how people believe they can improve their lives by rioting in the streets. Even though I played a part in what happened in the English colonies, I regard the results in America as an experiment. It remains to be seen whether that struggling new government will improve the conditions of its citizens, or for that matter, whether it will survive at all. King Gustav knew my loyalties. His orders were clear. I was to go to France and do whatever I could to help King Louis.

Fifteen years had passed since my first visit. I must admit, doubts crossed my mind more than once about how I would be received at Versailles. I need not have troubled myself. The formalities were observed by the full court. As personal emissary from King Gustav, I also received a private audience with King Louis. He was touched by Gustav's concern and gratified by the offer of help extended to him through me.

I knelt before My Queen. Her welcome was open and warm as to an old friend. As in the past, her eyes spoke directly to me. Nevertheless, it did not take long to realize the intervening years had made a difference. There was very little evidence of the defiance and recklessness that I remembered. Now she was much more aware of her responsibilities as Queen and as Mother. The sadness was still there in her eyes, but the cause was more obvious. The long-awaited heir was not a healthy child. The Queen was deeply concerned about the boy, and often tended to him herself. It seemed that she, and now King Louis too, both needed loyalty and friendship more than ever. As to the court, it was very much as I remembered it, if not more so, full of rumors, intrigue, and deceit.

I did my best to follow instructions from King Gustav with no success whatsoever.

It is true that Versailles was its own world. What I could not understand was the detachment of King Louis. If there was common knowledge in Sweden and in America about discontent among French citizens, how could it be that their own King could not anticipate the storms or foresee the danger?

The Dauphin, who was sickly for most of his eight years, died. Rather than signs of compassion and mourning during the child's solemn funeral cortege, I heard derisive shouts from his subjects. Even then the King did not see, or perhaps could not believe the depths of feeling against him and his wife. My sympathies were with the parents as they mourned. However, I was not so kindly disposed to the political inaction of the King. Through one crisis after another, he seemed to be unaware and did nothing.

Versailles itself was attacked by rioting mobs when the Queen's own bed was hacked by an ax. It was after that that the royal family and their attendants "for their own safety" were ordered to Paris. The orders came from the newly formed National Assembly. Not only did the Assembly dare to give orders to the King, the family was forced to leave the comfort and luxury of Versailles to the Tuileries, a dreary, uninhabited, cold, stone castle. Even at Tuileries where the King and Queen considered themselves to be prisoners, the King did not try to enlist my help or the help of other sympathizers. For two years or more, I observed and schemed and waited. For two painful years, I stood by, helpless.

What finally persuaded the King that it was too dangerous to remain in Paris, I do not know, but when he spoke to me, I was more than willing. At last something was to be done.

We come to the heart of my story.

I considered my first suggestions to the King and Queen for the escape to be quite sensible. We would keep all preparations secret; use smaller, light carriages which would be faster; travel in disguise; and with the least escort, try to attract as little attention as possible. This was not to be.

After much deliberation, it was finally decided the group for the journey was to be twelve in number: the King and Queen and their two children, a governess, a tutor, the King's sister, a valet to the King, two attendants to the Queen, and a cook, I was to be the twelfth.

The Queen insisted the family be kept together. I can understand this opinion from wife and mother, but there was no carriage to hold so many people. The compromise was one small carriage to hold young Charles who was now Dauphin, his governess, and the King's sister. I was to drive that carriage.

The other eight people were in a large, ornate carriage, very noticeable and cumbersome as well. It was also decided that a uniformed guard would provide escort. My suggestions to travel with discretion were ignored. Doubts come to me and I am harsh. Could I have been, or should I have been more forceful with the King and Queen? Yet, how does one give orders to a King and Queen, even for their own welfare, if they choose not to listen?

I can clearly recall my hopes for success as well as my fears of discovery. Every detail is fixed in my memory. The scene before me was so strange it has the quality of a dream if not a nightmare. It was night. Not a time when citizens of Paris would choose for a coach ride. Orders were given, and voices were hushed. Even the horses were unusually quiet. They and the coach were casting eerie shadows from the feeble light of one lantern.

Adding to the unreality were the passengers. There were the King and Queen of France disguised as ordinary citizens. There was ten year old Princess Teresa in a simple calico dress, and six year old Charles, the future King, dressed as a girl. Since the royal family must have its attendants, there were the others, I among them, clad as servants. In his innocence, I heard the boy ask if everyone was in costume for roles in a comedy.

My assignment was to provide arrangements only to Varennes. Varennes is northeast of Paris. It is not a port, but is close to the border of the Dutch. One of the many accusations against King Louis was that in that journey to Varennes, he was trying to escape from France. The King denied this accusation, and maintained until he died, that he only wanted for his family a safer refuge than Paris could provide. To my knowledge, the King had made no further arrangements.. Had there been such plans, palace rumors surely would have whispered the news. This I knew from experience.

Where royalty is concerned, nothing can be kept simple or secret. There are many to serve them in every chore from laying the fire to emptying the chamber pot. A lowly chambermaid, in the course of her duties, could hear snippets of conversation. Deviations from habit, changes in mood, or other telltale signs of preparation would be noticed. Servants, if they were so inclined, could repeat this information to interested parties either for politics or profit. Secrecy is difficult if not impossible.

From the outset of the preparations, I was especially concerned about the children, not only about their discretion, but also about their endurance. Even should everything work to our advantage, I estimated three long days of travel.

With the carriages open, the countryside would have provided some diversion for the entire company. As it was, the leather curtains were closed. It was June, quite warm, and therefore hot and stuffy within the carriage. The road was rutted, and the ride uncomfortable. But worse, nothing that was planned for the escape kept to its schedule. Horses pulling carriages tire. Teams of fresh horses to exchange were not in place as had been prearranged. The route was changed, and those involved were not always notified. When we stopped, it was more to rest or change the horses rather than to ease the passengers. Both adults and children under such conditions can be irksome and impatient.

As it developed, the children were not the problem. Both of them seemed to realize the seriousness of our adventure and acted accordingly. If the Princess in the other coach did become tiresome, it had no effect on the other passengers and was not reported to me.

The Dauphin was in my carriage. I saw his behavior for myself. He recited lessons to his governess, slept, amused himself with small toys, or chatted sensibly with the adults. It was during one of those times when he was absorbed, that he brushed back his long hair and exposed his right ear. It was then I saw his ear was malformed. In all other respects, the heir was handsome and well-built so that the image was a surprise and stayed with me. Years later when identifying the Dauphin became a matter of controversy, I was reminded of that unconscious gesture by the boy in the carriage that revealed his misshaped ear. But I wander from the matter at hand. In general as we rode toward our destiny, I was pleased with the boy's behavior and even enjoyed his company.

How could I have anticipated that it was the King himself who would give me most concern? It is not disloyalty, but honesty that compels me to admit the truth. It was the King's behavior that caused our discovery.

There were many carriages on the road to and from Paris. Other refugees leaving Paris traveled at will, usually without escort and mostly unnoticed. We were at a disadvantage. There was no doubt that someone important was traveling in our ornate coach with troops who were in uniform. However, the curtains were closed. Guesses could be made about the persons inside, but they would have been guesses, provided the King had been more prudent. Sadly, he was not. Time after time he allowed himself to be seen by whoever was around us, and there were always many who were tending to our needs.

How we were discovered was almost laughable. So many pieces of the puzzle fell into place at the wrong time, wrong for us, that is.

True, the King was disguised as an ordinary citizen. But he was a portly man with an easily recognizable figure with recognizable family features. Still he might have been taken for just another ordinary, portly man, except that Fate chose to interfere.

Our latest stop was at the town of St. Menehould whose postmaster, a man named Drouet with too good a memory for faces, just happened to be passing by. He saw the King and thought he recognized him. Any other man passing by might have been a little curious, observed the personage, and then gone about his business.

Not Drouet. As postmaster, he was an employee of the National Assembly and sympathetic to its cause. During the time the King was indecisive at Tuileries, this Assembly of citizens had grown in importance and in hostility to the King. Drouet understood the importance of his discovery. As our two coaches plodded on to Varennes, Drouet, on one horse at full speed, arrived in that town ahead of us. He had enough time not only to rouse officials of Varennes, but its citizens as well.

A disorderly crowd had gathered to greet our arrival. Boisterous debate developed as to whether or not it was the King. Some proof of his identity was necessary. When someone remembered the *assignat*, a coin issued by the Assembly with the image of this very King Louis standing before them, another piece of the puzzle fell into place. The likeness to the portly citizen before them was unmistakable. Thus it was that the King's own image was the instrument for discovery.

Even so, the crowd's reaction to the discovery of the King was mixed. For many it was no more than the curiosity of seeing an important personage. But Drouet, like a hunting dog who has cornered his prey, repeatedly agitated with threats that if the King were not returned to Paris, the entire town would pay a price. He continued his yapping and accusations until the crowd began to turn against the King.

This delay at Varennes was enough. Two officers sent by the Assembly to pursue our party, caught up with us. Their arrival was the final piece. Disheveled and dirty from the exertions of their rides, both men were overwrought with duties they must fulfill. Both men were taken to the King and Queen who were preparing for bed. The first officer presented his message from the Assembly to the King. It was an order. It demanded that the King and his party return to Paris immediately.

The second officer, this one in tears, held in his outstretched hand an edict from the Assembly. The King seized the paper in annoyance and read it quickly. He turned to the Queen. In a disgusted tone he announced, *"There is no longer a King in France!"* (3)

He threw the paper on the bed where his children lay, at which his wife picked it up and herself flung it on the floor exclaiming, *"I will not have it sully my children."*

By now both children were awake. Teresa whispered to her brother, *"Oh Charles, you were sadly mistaken; this is not a comedy."* To which Charles answered, *"I have perceived that long since."*

Instead of a successful escape, the royal party escorted by an angry mob, was forced to return to Paris. What should have been a turning point for the better for this family, was a turning point, but toward a Fate that horrifies me even now, a lifetime later.

From the outset, our escort on the return to Paris was unruly. As we passed through towns, we were joined by other citizens who grew in numbers and in hostility. They were prey to every rumor and acted on every angry thought.

In one town an official came to pay his respects to the King. As he was leaving the carriage, the official was seen to kiss the hand of the King. Some in the crowd saw this as a traitorous act and became infuriated. The mob seized the official from his horse, brutally killed him, and then mounted his head on a pike and carried it as a banner in front of the King's carriage.

At last we arrived in Paris. Posted in the streets were placards saying, *"He who cheers the king shall be beaten; he who insults him shall be hanged."* (4)

At the Tuileries, the very place from which our journey had begun, there was a crush of people at the gate. Heeding the signs, they were subdued and silent, but one could not help but notice: hats that would at other times be removed in respect as the King passed by, remained on heads. The whole of our return to Paris was frightening, but the silence at Tuileries seemed to be an added menace. It was then that the consequences of the failed escape hit full force in a terrible foreboding. In such an atmosphere, I could see nothing but evil in the future for My Queen, her children, the King and their future. The worst of it was that my part was done. I could do nothing more..

***

Long afterward I was told by someone that the Dauphin described our sad misadventure as a nightmare...a frightful dream in which he thought himself surrounded by ferocious beasts that sought to devour him. To me, Axel Fersen, the memory of those five days, the 20th through the 25th of June in 1791 is also a nightmare. I too, remember many ferocious beasts. But there is for me one primary villain, Drouet, an insignificant postmaster whose dogged single-mindedness bought him a shameful place in history.

I trust he does not rest in peace.

#

*Marie Antoinette and her two surviving
children before their imprisonment.
Teresa is on the left, Louis Charles on the right.*

Part II, The Palace at Versailles

May through October 1789

Excerpts from the journal of Baroness Elsa von Bradenberg, a fictional character.
Her observations are based on fact.

8 May 1789

How I long to have a hot bath! At Versailles, bathing is not a common practice, and I begin to understand the reasons. It has been an hour or more since I ordered the bath, and still I wait for water to be brought to my apartment. It seems to me to be a simple matter of carrying water from the kitchen, not at all a difficult task. Yet, by the time the lackeys bring the water, it is just tepid, and I am always annoyed.

Such laxity from servants should not be tolerated, but this is France. There is an undercurrent of defiance even in the king's own household. And so I am forced to adapt to what I would not accept in my father's house. Galling as it is, I have learned to use these hours of waiting to my advantage. I write in my journal.

I am at the court of King Louis XVI and Marie Antoinette in France at the behest of my Empress Maria Theresa (5) who is mother to Marie. The Empress was concerned. Marie's first son, the Dauphin, had been a sickly child for quite some time. Marie Antoinette and I have been friends since we were children together in Austria. The Empress seemed to think my presence as an old friendship might offer some comfort, and so I took residence at the palace of Versailles.

It was understood that by sending me to Versailles, the Empress would learn first hand about the welfare of her daughter and her family. I also know my Empress to be politic. It came as no surprise when she suggested that I keep her informed on matters developing in France. I can only do as my Empress bids, but in doing so, can I now be counted as a spy? It is a sobering thought. I am obligated to comply and reasoned a journal could be helpful.

11 May 1789

For years Versailles has been the envy of the courts of Europe for its luxury, its beauty, its fashions and its gaiety. Marie was known to contribute greatly to this reputation. Unfortunately, that Versailles is not the one that I am seeing. It is still a lavish court, but there is an atmosphere of suspicion and anxiety. As to Marie herself, motherhood and responsibility have taken their toll. The health of the Dauphin continues to decline. Marie is distracted with constant worry. I see only glimpses if the carefree, impetuous Marie that I remember from our youth.

15 May, 1789

Ah, the undercurrents and whisperings. Previously I valued the art of clever repartee. I still enjoy such exchanges, but now I find there is also merit to listening. It seems my childhood friendship with Marie does not grant immediate entry into the inner circle. Since I am new to court, my motives and loyalties are suspect. And so I listen. I hear enough to cause me much concern.

Marie is beset on all sides. There are the King's aunts. I've had slight exchange with them and wish to keep it at that. I see them as clucking hens with little interest or merit to what they have to say. The Queen's ladies are a nest of intrigue. They vie among themselves for favors from the Queen and offer small comfort in return. Marie's current favorite is Princesse de Lamballe who is superintendent of the Queen's household. She seems to be attentive to the Queen's wishes. As to loyalty, I cannot say. I must try to gain her confidence. The King's sister, Elizabeth, is more aloof than she is affectionate toward her brother's wife.

Worst of all are the King's two brothers. Each one thinks he would be a better king than Louis. Each has his own supporters. They work with rumors and lies to undermine their own brother and his wife in France and all of Europe. The most vicious rumor that is being attributed to one of them I heard even in

Austria. It is that King Louis is not father to his children. Since there were no children in the first seven years of marriage, too many are willing to believe this slander.

19 May 1789

A traitorous thought intrudes more often than I would wish. Is it possible the King's brothers are correct? That one of them might be a better king? I come by these doubts as I observe the King. At every opportunity someone is seeking the King's ear, even at table. One will say, "Your Majesty, last year's harvest was poor. Barns and warehouses are empty. The people are hungry. They need help." Another will say, "Sire, you must hold the reins tighter. There is looting and disorder."

Most often it is the vexing subject of taxes. Count Montaigne, whose family holds vast estates, holds surprising views. Frequently he tries to persuade the King that a small tax on those properties owned by the landed gentry and the Church would go far to appease the growing discontent. After he speaks, there is always a marked silence or mutterings of disapproval. His views are not well received. So it goes. The King needs to be a Solomon.

But sadly, the King is not a Solomon. Most often he responds with "We shall see," or "We will study it," and all without commitment. My father would have contempt for such inaction. He has often said that it is the duty of those in authority to make decisions. I have learned that some years past, the King tried to institute changes with very little success. It seems that now he has lost his appetite for action.

The King is however, more attentive to his supper than to his advisors. In this appetite he is near a glutton. At each sitting, vast quantities of food are placed before him and constantly replenished. Once (I will admit from vulgar curiosity) I noted that he consumed a whole roast chicken, several boiled eggs, a roast of beef, numerous preparations of vegetable accompaniments, two bottles of wine, and ending with a variety of pastries. I am amazed his girth is not greater than it is since he did not leave table to disgorge himself as the Romans did.

I can understand that Marie permits the attentions of the handsome Count

Fersen from Sweden. I'm told this is his second term of duty in France. His presence has revived the old rumors that it is more pleasure than duty on his part. Marie would do well to be more discreet. Does she not realize she is providing fodder for her enemies?

I must take pains to see these pages are well hidden.

25 May 1789

I was pleased to be included today to an excursion to Paris. It was far from the pleasant experience I had anticipated. As we neared the city, the streets became clamorous with agitators spewing their opinions, or by hawkers selling their printed papers, and each of them screeching in public places enough to deafen the ears. Count Dubois, our host, left our carriage several times to collect papers saying that he wished to keep informed about the doings of the rabble. The printed words he brought were unmistakable. Their intention was to rouse the citizens to action, even violence, against countless "injustices."

Another time when we stopped to allow another carriage to pass, an especially bold hawker forced his paper through the window. The moment was frightening not knowing if danger was to follow. Fortunately our driver whipped the horses and we escaped, though unnerved.

Nothing in the papers relieved our concerns. The worst was a cartoon in a gazette. It was a drawing of an ordinary citizen bent over double with his nose almost to ground. On his back were riding a priest and an aristocrat, as if the Church and nobility were a burden to citizens. It is no wonder there is discontent with such images being distributed among the people.

Another paper concentrated on the activities of the National Assembly organized only this month. The articles indicated this Assembly was composed of the Third Estate. In France this is a motley mixture of ordinary citizens and tradesmen. Apparently their intention is to make demands on the King's government. If they see themselves as downtrodden as the cartoon and articles suggest, who can predict what will be the extent of their demands?

The cartoon that troubled Elsa von Bradenburg.

A churchman (front figure), a noble (behind),

riding on the back of an ordinary man

29 May 1789

Since my arrival, I have been puzzled by how little affection or respect the court has toward Marie. After fifteen years as their Queen, whispers still refer to her as the Austrian. Worse, there are constant snide and suggestive remarks about the relationship with two of her ladies, and, should any courtier, including Count Fersen, pay the slightest attention to her, rumors begin to fly immediately. Yet, there are signs of affection between the King and Queen.

Today I chanced on the King's sister strolling alone in the gardens. I seized on the opportunity for conversation hoping she would permit the intrusion. Who better than Elizabeth to shed some light on Marie's early years in France? I made a comment on the beauty of the garden design and on the glory of the day. She answered graciously, and we fell into step It was the usual social chatter until I mentioned how impressed with Versailles Marie must have been at her arrival here.

Elizabeth responded with an unmistakable, "Humph!" and a short pause, then, "One would think so, but I'm inclined to believe she was more intent on impressing the court with her own importance."

Those words were the beginning to a number of disapproving observations about Marie:

That the family had expected a more sophisticated princess. Instead they were disappointed that she was a silly and superficial young girl.

That her education was sorely lacking. She could barely read. I was about to ask if Elizabeth meant in French or in her own German, but Elizabeth continued.

That Elizabeth and the aunts tried to guide Marie, but she rejected their suggestions.

That Marie was vain and self-centered.

At this I asked about Louis' reaction to his betrothed. I was told he was shy and not as assertive as he should have been. Even after they were married and he assumed the throne, he was indulgent toward her whims. She pointed to a lovely small palace, and said the Petit Trianon was an unwise gift from Louis to his bride. It became a hideaway for Marie and her friends. Their wild and careless behavior there prompted stories that were quick to spread. At the end of our conversation, Elizabeth did concede that when the children came, Marie was more maternal than anyone expected her to be.

I gained more insight than I would have wanted. Reluctantly I had to admit that the gist of what Elizabeth told me was not difficult to believe. Marie and I were both sixteen years old when our paths parted. I was betrothed and soon married to a kind man and stayed within the comfort of the familiar, while

Marie was thrust as a stranger and alone into unfamiliar ground and into what I would consider the politics of a mean court.

As I remember it, she and I were equally naïve and no doubt as silly and imprudent as Elizabeth describes. It is also true that our lessons were in social skills, duty and obedience, certainly not challenging or enlightening subjects. Further, Marie was always conscious of her rank. She was not at all inclined to listen to any tutor or governess who might offer some criticism of her. I began to understand. It would be Marie's nature, when she was alone and afraid, to hide behind the shield of arrogance and pride.

Apparently in this court, Marie could expect no understanding or forgiveness for such youthful thoughtlessness.

7 June 1789

The Dauphin died three days ago. He was eight years old. That the heir to any throne should die is no small matter. Versailles, Paris, and I suppose all of France have assumed the appearance of mourning. I choose the word 'appearance' deliberately. For the most part, Versailles and its grounds and gardens is an island. For that reason the carriage ride to and from the service at the cathedral was most disturbing. Even on this solemn occasion, there were disrespectful and ugly shouts against the king and queen: "Good riddance!" "God's punishment on you!" "Go back to Austria!" I am appalled at such behavior from citizens. The militia should have cleared the streets and spared the King and Queen this added anguish.

Marie is distraught. This is her second child to die. I try to understand her pain and loss. I trust that I am of some comfort and consolation to my friend during her sorrow.

15 June 1789

Marie of course mourns her son, though she and the king take comfort from the two who survive. The daughter, Teresa, is ten years old and shows some promise of beauty and charm.

Louis Charles, known simply as Charles, is four years old and is an appealing child. He has a sturdy little body, chestnut colored curls, blue eyes fringed with long reddish lashes, a fair complexion, and a dimple in his chin. On those fair days when we are in the garden, Charles is often romping with his little dog, Moufflet, that I am told he inherited from his brother along with his title of Dauphin.

Since he is now the heir to the throne, I was curious about his nature. On several occasions, I made an effort to speak directly to the boy. Surprisingly, I found myself in sensible conversation rather than hearing just the childish prattle of a four-year-old. He invited me to see the small flower garden that he himself tends, and assumed the manner of a courtier. Then nodding seriously, he said, "Every morning I pick the prettiest blossom and take it to Mamma. I like to see her smile. She's sad now."

I was quite charmed and reported my experience to Marie. She in turn told me of a mischievous incident. Young Charles took it upon himself to hide the flute of a page at court. To teach the boy a lesson, Marie blamed Moufflet for hiding the flute and punished the dog by shutting him in a cupboard. On learning this, Charles was overcome with remorse, confessed that he was the culprit, took the punishment for the dog, and then returned the flute to the page. Marie and I both were amused and pleased. It seems to me that such a story, childish prank though it was, speaks well to the character of the Dauphin.

20 June 1789

These past weeks have been difficult for the entire court as well as the parents. The King added to the Queen's distress on a matter of medicine. On his insistence, he, Marie and the children were to be vaccinated against smallpox. This vaccination is a controversial procedure that actually introduces the dreadful pox into the body. It was especially frightening to Marie who knew well enough that the King's grandfather had died from smallpox, and that for three years, this inoculation was banned in France. Of course she was fearful that her children should be exposed to such danger. Nevertheless they were inoculated. Thankfully there were no lasting ill effects except for a scar on the Dauphin's arm. The scar was not unsightly, but quite obvious on his unblemished skin.

25 June 1789

I have sent several letters to the Empress. In them I related observations about Marie and her children that I thought would interest a mother and grandmother. I have only recently received a reply. Her Esteemed Majesty hinted somewhat less than tactfully, that I should apply myself less to chestnut curls, little dogs, and childish pranks and more to matters of substance. Henceforth to reflect her wishes, I will be more attentive to such matters.

15 July 1789

The court is most disturbed at news of the attack on the Bastille yesterday. There are many who believe this to be the beginning of the revolution to overthrow the monarchy. I cannot believe this deed to hold such importance. The Bastille is an old prison with few prisoners in it. It cannot be considered a victory for an angry mob to overcome those few soldiers left as guards. Yet it seems the influence of this action has spread from Paris to the countryside. It is as if the fall of the Bastille has affected the very atmosphere, and I must admit, this atmosphere is frightening. I have tried to collect some explanation as to why this raid holds such importance.

Many people through the years were held prisoners in its dungeons, often without trial. Therefore the Bastille is a symbol of injustice. Further, weapons and ammunition stored in the Bastille are now in the hands of lawless rabble who previously were armed only with pitchforks and knives. With weapons, the so-called Third Estate now feels its power. That feeling of power is contagious.

Most troubling of all, I am told the King's minister of war informed the King that his own army may not be willing or able to protect Versailles or the monarchy. If this is true, it may very well signal the beginning of the end.

There is a possibility that the King could negotiate some agreement with the Assembly. I see this possibility as remote. Even when the King is decisive, he is not given to compromise. Nor should he be. He is the King.

August 1789

The so-called leaders of the National Assembly have occupied themselves with proclamations instead of attacks. The Assembly has issued the Declaration of the Rights of Man and Citizen. I am told it lists all manner of entitlements due to commoners. Could people really believe such wishful pronouncements?

8 October 1789

I made some slight notes in my journal these past months, but nothing of import. Perhaps I was not as observant as I should have been. I regret to say the calm was deceptive. It may very well have endangered our lives. We were completely unprepared, and barely survived two nights of terror.

The first night on 5 October was frightening enough, but still did not prepare us for what was to come. On that first night, Versailles was assaulted by an unruly, ragamuffin mob of mostly women who were crying for bread and demanding to see the King.

I had of course seen poor women and shabby vendors in the streets. Here among the riches of the palace, the contrast was shocking. The women were in ragged or dirty clothes with haggard faces, some carrying crying infants, or holding older children by the hand, and all of them unkempt, crude, and noisy. But it was their cries that I remember most. Again and again we heard the words "Bread!" "Bread!" in piteous or frightening voices.

When the King bravely went to speak to them (he showed more courage than I had), they quieted enough to listen to his words. He told them he would order the granaries to be opened so they could have flour. At that their desperation seemed to ease. A few thanked him and some even cheered. Gradually the women began to disperse though noisily, with chattering and shoving and gawking and pointing at their surroundings. The ending was peaceful, but I do admit, it was an altogether fearsome experience.

Among ourselves, we asked, what was it that drove these common women to the palace? And why did they demand bread of the King? It was a puzzle until very soon, an evil rumor reached our ears. It was that the women believed the King and his nobles were deliberately hoarding grain for their own use. Imagine! It is a revelation to me that the common people are so willing to believe the worst of those above them.

This first night of mischief, as disrupting as it was, was not enough. The agitators were not satisfied. The forces of hate regrouped for a second night of terror. This time it was not mostly women, but hundreds of ruffians and thugs, filled with hatred and bent on violence. They were armed with all manner of clubs, knives, hatchets, and some firearms. We were driven from our beds with shouting and great disturbances. This very likely saved us.

It was very early morning when the ruffians broke through the palace gates. We heard the shouting mob and thud of boots along the corridor to the Queen's apartment, and then the cries of men in the heat of killing, and the screams of two queen's guards, helpless against the numbers, as they were butchered. When the invaders discovered the Queen was gone from her chamber, in frustrated rage, they chopped to pieces her bed that was still warm from her body. She had escaped only minutes before.

With my own eyes, I saw the King clutch the Dauphin in his arms and run toward a secret passageway, the boy's little dog so close at his feet as to nearly trip the King. In this way the King saved himself and the child.

Count Fersen was absent from the palace. I chanced to meet him later when he questioned me about both nights. I related in detail the harrowing experiences. He was deeply concerned at the escalation in violence, and could not understand why the King did not take some action to escape. Then reluctantly he told me of a troubling rumor about Marie that had spread like a fire gone wild. What he heard on the streets was that when the women marched on Versailles crying for bread, the Queen's answer was, "Let them eat cake!"

It was obvious that he was troubled by this rumor. I reassured him that it was a wicked lie. I was present and an observer throughout the confrontation. The Queen did not speak, and even so, could not have made such a heartless remark. It is as if during these times, there is no one willing to remember acts of charity or kindness from their Queen or from their King.

Though many lost their lives, we did survive, but no sense of comfort and security is left to us. Our lives are altered..

The National Assembly acted quickly. Using the guise of safety for the royal family, the Assembly "recommended" that the King's household be removed to Paris to an aged castle, the Tuileries. The truth was, the King had no choice except to acquiesce. Imagine!

As for me, I have my suspicions of these new arrangements. Although the Queen expressly asked that I be permitted to accompany the family to the Tuileries, this was not allowed by whoever are these new powers of the National Assembly that can override royal wishes.

Therefore this is my last entry. I am requesting permission from Her Esteemed Majesty to return to Austria. I greatly fear what is in store for France and for my friend.

#

Part III, THE TUILERIES

October 1789 through September 1792
(Except for five days)
As told by Gerard Gascon, a fictional character who was a member
of the National Guard.
The events are historically accurate.

I heard them before they came into view. It was as if a violent storm cloud was approaching, shapeless, yet dark and threatening. As the cloud neared, I was able to make out a multitude of bodies, both men and women brandishing pikes, tools, guns, knives or anything else that could serve as a weapon. Many were drunk and using language that would have put our barracks to shame. But whether drunk or not, all were disheveled, raucous, and disorderly.

It was not at all what I had prepared for. I was to be a part of the unit to welcome the royal family in its move from Versailles to the Tuileries palace in Paris. I had heard of the glories of Versailles and should have noticed the condition of the Tuileries which was in disrepair and dismal. That such a place was considered to be suitable for the king and his family should have given me some hint of what was to come.

But I was nineteen years old, proud to be a part of the National Guard, and quite taken with the uniform. The black cutaway coat and red vest drew admiring glances from girls, while I tried not to be aware that the white, closely fitted trousers showed off my legs to an advantage. I cleaned the brass buttons, polished my black boots to a high gloss, and prepared myself for the ceremonies. No doubt I was as self-absorbed as any young man could be, but even if I had been more aware, nothing could have prepared me for the approach of the king's party and their "escort".

A large part of the spectacle was the corps of the King's private Guard. I later learned there were about two hundred men. Their elegant uniforms were in disarray and stained with blood and soil. Each Guardsman was being buffeted by two citizens who carried weapons while the Guardsmen themselves were disarmed and dispirited. It was a shock to see.

Even more shocking were the heads of two Guardsmen killed at Versailles that were mounted on pikes and flaunted. When I saw the heads with their staring eyes, mouths frozen in agonized grimaces, and the necks still trailing gore, the gorge began rising in my throat, and I nearly disgraced myself before my comrades.

Amidst this inhumanity rode the king's carriage. It must have been prophetic that I thought of the two children inside the carriage for I was to see them often as part of my duties at the Tuileries.

The mayor of Paris met the king's carriage as it approached the garden of the Tuileries. The mayor greeted the party with polite words of welcome and hoped that Paris would become the king's permanent residence. The king replied, *"It is ever with pleasure and confidence that I find myself among the inhabitants of my good city of Paris."(6)*

I, who was near enough to hear this exchange of greetings, could hardly believe my ears. Both the king and the mayor were acting as if this move to Paris were a royal choice when it was obvious, even to me, that the mob had done the deciding.

The spectacle that day left its mark. The sorry procession I had witnessed created a seed of doubt. If I thought of them at all, I had rarely questioned my father's views. Now I began to question ideas I had heard all my life.

From the earliest times that I can remember, our home was a gathering place. That in itself was not unusual. What was unusual, was that my father, a wine merchant, allowed his children after a certain age, to join adult company. Whether it was a social occasion or business, we children could be present as long as we did not intrude in any way.

Our visitors were mostly tradesmen of every variety. What brought these men together was that they all thought changes needed to be made in the way France was governed. The Church and the aristocracy, for some reason known as the First and Second Estates, had all the power. The Third Estate, that is everyone else, my father included, thought that because of their numbers, they should at the least have some voice. My father and his friends became representatives to the National Assembly. The idea was that perhaps they might have some influence on the king and his advisers.

It was not that my older brother and I were particularly interested in these men, or that we even listened attentively. For us it was entertainment. The conversation (and gossip, too) was lively, but when the talk turned to politics, it was sure to get livelier. Quite often one of the men would arrive agitated or angry. Then my brother and I made sure we were present when sparks flew.

Once a shopkeeper stomped into our salon fuming that some Marquis or other was an idiot: that he knew nothing about business, yet had the power to decide what could or could not be done; that he had no ability or ideas and only kept his position because he had a title; that he cared nothing for business, only to preserve his own privileges!

I had been taught to respect titles. The opinions in the shopkeeper's outburst were new to me then, but more and more we heard such complaints.

Another time a simple farmer came with hat in hand. His manner was meek, but his words sputtered with anger. He told us that three times already, hunting parties of nobles on horses had trampled his crops. The last time just at harvest when a field of crops was ruined.

One of the men there reminded the farmer that aristocrats had the right to hunt on any land. The farmer pleaded before my father's group. They had to do something to change the laws. He had a family to feed!

Whatever was the subject of the meeting, almost always the discussion turned to unfair taxes. Over and over we heard that the church and nobility owned great properties. They paid no taxes either on them or on the income from them. It was everyone else, my father and these men, who were being taxed more and more. And who was it that passed the laws? The very ones who paid no taxes at all. Young as I was, I knew this was injustice.

Wine growers who dealt with my father complained of the tax they had to pay for pressing the grapes. But everyone agreed the worst tax of all was the one put on the mills that ground the grain into flour. That tax affected everyone who ate bread.

A man came in one evening, poured himself a glass of wine (I suspect not his first), sat on the floor in the middle of the room, and explained he heard these words from street vendors in the market. In a mocking, sing-song fashion, he began to recite:

"A tithe to the church, a tax on income,
a tax on each person, a tax on salt,
forced labor on roads, cash rent to the lord,
and a tax on property sold."

My brother and I got the giggles that immediately produced a severe look from my father, and a hand gesture that banished us. It was just as well. Outside the room, we continued to giggle helplessly and chanted the list to each other so that I remember it to this day. We liked the rhythm of the words.

It was here also that I first learned of the exploits of the Marquis de Lafayette, the commanding officer of my National Guard. He was a hero in France because he had helped the American colonies defeat the English. There had never been sympathy from Frenchmen for English problems. This time France paid heavily and even went into debt to help the Colonies defeat England. Now the people were being squeezed even more to pay for this involvement.

Very often, the queen was also a part of the conversation. She was referred to as "the Austrian" or "that woman" or worse. Usually there was some uncomplimentary story… sometimes in whispers and with laughter among the men.

Once I overheard that the queen was very fond of some madame or other and was seen kissing her. At this there were snickers and shaking of heads which I did not understand. In our family it was common for women and their friends to kiss one another. But the whisperings, winks, and hints had an effect. I did not have a fondness for the queen.

These are views that I heard constantly. I absorbed them through repetition. My father and his friends hoped that changes could be made gradually through the National Assembly. When the king made vague promises that were often ignored; when the nobles thwarted any changes at all; when the conditions in the country continued to worsen, more and more cautious people like my father became increasingly radical. There was less talk of the rights of kings and more talk of the rights of citizens, and devil take any nobility that got in the way.

Still I suppose that what I had learned in my father's house had for the most part prepared me to expect righteous grievances expressed with at least a degree of reason and civility. The mob surrounding the king on his return to the Tuileries, were such views run completely amok. What I saw from the citizens in that procession was an unleashed fury that disturbed me to my very roots.

***

Since the Tuileries had not been in use for one hundred years or more, there was little in the way of necessities and nothing in the way of comfort or beauty in the furniture or hangings. When the royal family entered, the dauphin spoke my very thoughts when he said, *"Everything is very ugly here, mamma."*

The queen answered her son with *"My dear, Louis the XIV lived here, and found it comfortable; we must not be more fastidious than he."*(7)

Her words took me aback. They seemed like those my mamma would use in chiding my own little brother. The queen's words were not at all what I expected.

The royal family had been remote personages. Now I saw them almost daily, and my curiosity increased. Sometimes I could observe incidents for myself, and other times I learned from barracks talk or from conversations in the kitchen of the Tuileries, for all of us took interest in the doings of our charges. Our orders were to protect all members of the king's party. One or more of us was with them at all times. The word was not spoken, but they may as well be called our prisoners.

The princess Teresa was a coltish girl. I saw her least of all and truthfully, she did not take my interest. There were also valets, ladies-in-waiting, tutors, governesses and companions. On some occasions they engaged us in conversation, but only of necessity.

The Dauphin however, was cheerful and friendly and curious and, with or without his little dog, always in motion. In one of our first encounters, I asked him his age. He looked up at me in great seriousness and proudly announced, "*I am almost five!*" His manner was exactly that of my youngest brother who was a nuisance more often than not, but whose dogged attentions I seemed to miss.

On one occasion young Charles was in my particular charge on a visit with his governess to a nearby estate. Here there were other children and space to play. In a game of Hide and Seek, Charles ran off. When next I saw him, he was at the top of a tottering ladder against a hayloft.

My heart began pounding its way out of my body. I was sure he would fall, but the ladder steadied. The future king of France, with an impish grin of satisfaction, triumphantly counted his steps as he descended the ladder. My relief was monumental. I could only imagine my fate had the child been hurt. Had he indeed been my little brother, I would have given the scamp a reminder on his bottom for making such a reckless climb and causing me distress.

Despite his little boy behavior, an abbe who was tutor to the dauphin arrived daily. Since my little brother at this age had no schooling, I was curious as to what the prince was being taught. I was never a scholar, but the subjects offered to this child were more than my entire education. Besides lessons in tennis and dancing, he was studying arithmetic, geography, history, religion, writing, and most surprisingly, botany.

I was told that at Versailles the boy had his own little garden that he sorely missed. In the spring after his arrival at Tuileries, a small plot was provided for him. Young as he was, Charles had great patience in his work and the plants seemed to thrive under his care. By summer he often favored a guard with a blossom. He bestowed the flower in the manner of a gracious monarch. We could be knighted with the same dignity and ceremony.

His manner was both endearing and amusing as when he practiced with his little wooden musket. It seemed to me our drills improved after we saw the boy mimic our moves. Once when he, with his musket, was leaving the chateau, I was on duty. In a manner that I had intended as jest, I said to him, *"Monsigneur, as you are going out, surrender me your musket."* At these words, not in keeping with his usual courtesy, he refused, obstinately and with great indignation.

When the governess scolded him for his rudeness, the prince answered, *"If the gentleman had said: give me your musket, that would have been very well, ---but surrender it!"* (8) Already he understood the difference between 'give' and 'surrender.' He spoke like a king. There was no doubt that he was a royal.

Since I had little regard for the queen, I thought her charitable acts were more for public display than genuine. But time and time again, I or other guards, accompanied the queen to hospitals or foundling homes or even to a private cellar or garret. The queen offered words of comfort and coins to those in need, but more important, she gave her attention to their misery.

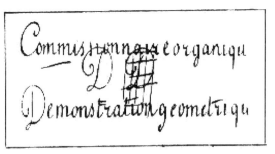

The Dauphin's handwriting before he was imprisoned, when he was five years old.

The Dauphin's signature as a witness against his mother, three years later.

Charles was often her companion on these visits. His interest was especially for the foundling hospital. Of course I did not see it then, but when I recall those visits, it was as if Charles had a premonition of his own fate. He brought flowers from his garden, but also saved coins from his own pocket money to dispense. More than once I heard him ask, *"Mamma, when shall we come back again?"* (9) It appeared to me that his deepest sympathy was with those children who were orphans.

France was in continual turmoil. Leaders, policies, and laws were constantly being changed in hopes something would make a difference. Nothing did. The economy did not improve and consequently the forces of disruption were gaining ground. Yet at Tuileries, we maintained our usual routines until the week of Easter. After that, nothing was the same.

It started when the king wanted a change from dreary Tuileries and decided the family would attend Easter services at the nearby parish of St. Cloud. There was nothing unusual about the decision until the suspicions of politics interfered.

The Assembly had recently taken severe action. It had confiscated all properties of the Church and, to add to the treasury, was selling these properties. Many including clergy, considered this to be a necessary change. The Assembly however, was not satisfied. It became even more assertive and issued another declaration. All Church officials were declared to be under the authority of the government and had to swear allegiance to the state. This declaration was far more drastic.

By coincidence at that same time, the King just happened to make two decisions. He dismissed the priest who was his confessor and also wanted to visit St. Cloud. Rumors did the rest. The suspicions against the king were so intense that he was accused of defying the law in two ways. That the King had dismissed his confessor because the priest had taken the oath of loyalty to the new government, and further, that the king disobeyed the new law by wanting to attend a disloyal parish where the priest had not taken the oath.

The royal party was already in the carriage when hundreds gathered and would not allow the carriage to leave. For two hours the Guard, I among them, fended off assaults from this unruly crowd, fearing for our lives and for the lives of our charges within the carriage. And none of this near violence based on any truth.

This harrowing experience changed the very climate at the Tuileries. Whatever easiness had grown between our charges and ourselves was gone. After every outing we escorted them to their apartments on pretext that we were an honor guard. At night guardsmen were on pallets outside their separate doors. The royals were, now in fact, our prisoners.

Nevertheless, it happened. During the night of June 20, 1791, in my second year of duty with the Guard, two months after the carriage debacle, despite our constant and greater precautions, the royal family somehow managed to escape through secret passages in the Tuileries. Their escape was not spontaneous and caused consternation everywhere: among the Guard, within all Tuileries, and certainly in the Assembly which did for once act decisively. As soon as members could assemble on the day after the escape, two decrees, both regarding the king, were issued. Lafayette was charged with their delivery to the king and assigned two officers to the task. When the officers caught up with the royal party in Varennes in early morning, the king's party was set to begin its forced return. I learned later that Count Fersen of Sweden orchestrated the escape.

Sometime during this period, the Assembly also abolished hereditary titles. To me it seemed unnatural and even disrespectful to refer to everyone, regardless of position, merely as 'citizen.'

Again I was witness to the arrival of the King's carriage to Tuileries. Again the carriage was accompanied by raucous citizens. The difference this time was that it was no longer King, Queen, Dauphin and Princess, but rather it was simply Citizen Louis Capet and his wife and children. The throngs waiting at the gate reflected these new conditions and showed no outward signs of respect.

Circumstances now at Tuileries were entirely different. I no longer enjoyed my duties in the Guard, and the uniform did not compensate. The business of selling wine, to my own surprise, began to have appeal, and I resigned from the Guard. This pleased my father more than I would have thought, since previously he had not much confidence in my practical sense. But I must admit, three years in a young man's life will sometimes provide different perspectives.

***

The civilian world of commerce was intertwined with politics. It was necessary that I be informed to keep abreast of those who made decisions affecting our trade. I became more knowledgeable about the workings of the revolution and the changes in its course. And so I read whatever came to hand and even joined my father's group at times.

Though their opinions were diverse, these men were well informed and their information was reliable. They were most concerned about the growing strength of the Jacobins, a political club that had started much like my father's, but had developed far more attention and influence.

The Jacobins had within their ranks two rising stars: Maximilien Robespierre who did become a leader during what came to be called the "Reign of Terror." It was already beginning though we did not know it; and Jean Paul Marat, an extremist writer of the first order, whose newspaper spewed venom and advocated violence upon any who opposed the revolution. In Marat's writings, his were the only righteous views. *"Let the blood of the traitors flow,"* (10) he ranted. Unfortunately too many took his words to heart. Acts of such violence that reasonable people cannot explain, were frequent and common.

Through a former barracks' companion, Henri Pardeau, I was able to keep informed about the welfare of the royal family, especially young Charles. It was through Henri that I learned of the first senseless event that took place at the Tuileries.

In the early morning of 20th June, citizens, for whatever reasons, began to collect until it was a multitude of thousands of bodies who were milling through the streets. By noon the mob invaded the Tuileries and rampaged through the castle room by room.

As Henri related, the royal family and their attendants were caught in separate apartments with no comfort from each other as they were confronted with abuse, humiliation, and threats. There were repeated cries of, *"Send out their heads!"* and *"Death to the tyrants!"*(10) throughout the rioting in garden and castle.

One man armed with a pike cried, *"Where is he that I may kill him?"* At these words Henri, who till now had been powerless against the numbers, threw down the man at the feet of the king and forced him to say, *"Vive le Roi!"* (11)

But Henri could do nothing to prevent another man, with bottle and glass in hand, who demanded the king drink a toast to the nation. Henri was aghast as the king drank, not knowing what was in the bottle.

The queen was separated from her husband and quite often from her children. She found young Charles just as the intruders were pounding on the apartment door. She saved them both by barely escaping into a secret passage. As they cowered inside, they heard the sounds of hatchets splintering wood just outside the door behind which they were concealed.

In the evening of that long and frightening day, the mayor of Paris at last was able to speak to the crowd and asked them to return to their homes. Gradually they did begin to disperse.

There was no worthwhile result from this upheaval except that Lafayette let it be known almost immediately that such extreme actions were not acceptable. He demanded that the Assembly identify and punish the leaders. Since not much was done by the Assembly to honor his rank and comply with his orders, he resigned as commander of the Guard soon thereafter and altogether quit his work for the revolutionary cause.

The constant ravings of Marat and his ilk continued to goad the people. Abuse and threats were not enough. There was a thirst for blood. Somewhere almost continuously during August and September of that same year, there were mayhem, murder and destruction. But two events deserve greater attention: the first because it had an impact on the royal family and on history, as well as for its carnage; the second only for its senseless carnage.

In all the general disturbances, there were increasing demands to depose the king and deprive him of official powers, though I would argue that he had not many left. Affairs of business being muddled and uncertain, I went often to the Assembly in hopes that I would gain some information that was useful.

Instead what I heard were endless hours of speakers railing against the crimes committed by the King. The decision was finally made that the King was to be brought before the Assembly on August 10, 1789. That was the day he would be stripped of all his authority.

In preparation for that fateful day both sides gathered at the Tuileries. Aligning in the courtyard as supporters of the Assembly, were thousands of people. They were individually armed with various weapons, but there were canon as well. Aligning inside the castle for the King and his family were a mere handful of remaining friends, and some National Guard, Henri among them. These paltry few ... against the thousands amassing in the courtyard.

Early on the morning of August 10th, an official perceived the hopeless odds. He recognized that there was no safety possible for the royal family at Tuileries. In desperation he suggested to them that the National Assembly itself might provide the only safe haven.

The queen cried, "...*you propose to us to seek refuge among our most cruel persecutors? Never!...But say, Sir, are we utterly abandoned?*" (12) There it was. She spoke the words of stark reality.

Still the queen demanded from the official that he guarantee the lives of her son and husband. To which the official replied, "*Madame, we answer for dying at your side; that is all we can guarantee.*"

The courtyard that the family had to cross to the Assembly was not great, but the crossing took near half an hour through the press of shoving and pulling bodies shouting insults and threats. A guardsman carried the dauphin and tried to ease his fears by saying, "*Do not be afraid. They will do you no harm.*" But Charles could see the obvious and said, "*Not to me, perhaps, but to my father!*" (13) They were brought inside before the Assembly. The drama was coming to an end, and I stayed to witness the proceedings.

It was one of the hottest days of August in a space packed to overflowing with humanity (and some not quite so human). The royal family was placed in the lowliest seats in a confined space where no breath of air could reach.

The Assembly hall itself was noisy with people coming and going, though it was not easy to do so. There were private conversations of the spectators and the members, and orators striving to be heard. With all that tumult inside the hall, we still could hear the attack cries of assassins and the screams of their victims coming from the courtyard and nearby Tuileries, Within Tuileries, the rampaging mob had no control or law. It vented its fury on draperies and furniture and people without regard or mercy. Henri saved himself by hiding in a kitchen pot.

These horrors were out of sight and left to the imagination. The other horror was within the Assembly Hall. Looters (some covered in blood) placed on a table before the president, silver, jewels, and personal belongings pillaged from those in the castle. These thefts were presented triumphantly as prizes. Worse, the thieves were praised for their success. Here I was overcome with disgust! Where is law? What excuses will history make for the authorities within the Hall who are supposedly upholding the law and yet do nothing when laws are broken?

Spectacle though it was, the appearance of the royal family before the Assembly was not a trial. This meeting was to justify the act of removing all power from the king. For two full days, within their sweltering nook, the royals sat through the harangues against them. At the end of the second day, the deed was done. There were of course official documents to come, but one simple phrase "…*the revocation of the authority entrusted to Louis XVI*" *(14)* proclaimed that King Louis XVI and his wife, Marie Antoinette were no longer King and Queen of France.

While the horrible smell of burning bodies (which had to be disposed of in the August heat) wafted into the hall, there was more discussion as to what place was suitable custody for the Capet family. When I finally heard The Temple was selected, my spirits sank. The name comes from its history and is deceptive. I knew it for what it was… in fact as barren, cold, and stony as any prison. I feared for what was to become of them. The last time I saw any member of the Capet family was as they were being taken away. My attention was on Charles. I will never forget the look upon this child's face.

***

The bloodletting did not abate. There was continuing senseless carnage. Less than a month later, some 1200 prisoners were slaughtered during "The September Massacres" as it came to be known. Many of the prisoners were clergy who rejected the oath to the state, or other minor criminals. They were murdered in their cells and on prison grounds because they were suspected of "plotting to overthrow the government."

Years later I came across this account of what the prisoners endured:

"The most important matter that employed our thoughts was to consider what posture to adopt when we were dragged to the place of slaughter, in order to suffer death with the least pain. Occasionally we asked some of our companions to go to the window to watch the attitude of victims. They came back to say that those who tried to protect themselves with their hands suffered the longest, because the blows of the knives were thus weakened before reaching the head; that some of the victims actually lost their hands and arms before their bodies fell; and that those who put their hands behind their backs obviously suffered less pain. We, therefore, recognized the advantage of this last posture and advised each other to adopt it when it came our turn to be butchered." Jourgniac de Saint-Meard, Abbaye Prison (15)

There is one final note to my narrative. I have come to believe that when fury is unleashed, it can lose direction and change course. So it was with Jean-Paul Marat. I admit a perverse satisfaction when I learned how he had died. Within the year, Marat was killed by one Charlotte Corday, who took his teachings to heart. She stabbed him to death while he was in his bath.

***

And so it was in time, my father's teachings lost their hold. In my heart I understood the grievances of the republican cause maintained by my father and his friends in the Assembly. My concern was with the cures they proposed. I did not see their cures as being more just or humane than what they were protesting against.

#

Part IV, The Temple

August 10, 1792 through June 10, 1795
As told by Turgy (16) who was a cook at Versailles, Tuileries, and The Temple.
His words are the author's invention. The information is historically accurate.

A bowl of soup, a cup of ale, the comfort of a kitchen all work wonders to loosen tongues. These small attentions I have always permitted wherever I was cook. Thus it was I learned my King and his family arrived at The Temple with nothing: not money, not toiletries, not even a change of linen, and with young Charles, the Dauphin, crying for the little dog he had not seen since the family was taken from the Tuileries.

During those two days after Tuileries was ransacked and the King was humiliated in the Assembly, I acted. By hook and by crook, I managed to secure the position as cook at The Temple, perhaps in some way to be helpful to my King.

My private fancy is that my fortunes and my King's are parallel. When I rose from undercook to that of chief cook, he rose from dauphin to king, both of us at Versailles. Likewise, in his decline from Versailles to Tuileries to Temple, I followed. Among the many obvious differences between us, one of the most important is that my decisions were my own, while his were thrust upon him.

I wonder at myself and at the path I chose. What bonds of loyalty could exist between a cook and king? My answer is perhaps not from him to me, but my loyalty to him is strong and came about through accident of living.

I first came to Versailles on the verge of manhood, but rootless, as the lowliest in the scullery to scrub the cooking pots. To me this was improvement in my life. There was food to eat and warmth in winter, though admittedly in summer there was more heat than I needed. I may have been there still except for a serious bout of illness. The kitchen staff had few left to work, and the King and his court must be fed. The chief cook caught sight of me, a body that was moving, and put me to work under strict direction. I took this as opportunity and did my best to do as I was told. As some returned to work and some did not, I kept my temporary place.

There was a cook's assistant who saw my willingness to learn and coached me in small ways so that my skills increased. In time I learned all complicated parts of preparing food and found I loved the work. But more, I loved the atmosphere of being at the heart, and, the kitchen was the heart of Versailles. Not only was the King a great consumer of all that we prepared, but not much occurred within the court that the kitchen did not learn. We were a part of all that was important at Versailles.

I was a second cook when Marie Antoinette came from Austria to wed Louis Auguste who was Dauphin and not yet King. We prepared a lavish wedding feast, which did honor to France. As reward for extraordinary work, we cooks, ourselves, served several courses so that we could take some small part in the celebration.

In serving her, I saw for the first time the princess in all her wedding finery. She was but fifteen years old with quite a pretty face. She had not the beauty of a full-formed woman, though the makings of beauty were there. The splendor of her costume emphasized her youth. She seemed a doll of wax animated only at brief moments, though she was more animated than the Dauphin, in equal splendor beside her. My heart went out to both for what they must endure.

I was already married and learned through error that marriage was more than a tumble in the hay. My lessons I learned in private. The Dauphin and Princess had not the luxury of privacy. Their every act was scrutinized by the court, even to the sheets of their wedding bed being examined for evidence that the marriage was consummated. Unfortunately, no such evidence was produced, and grounds for rumors and suspicion were created. Unlikely as it may seem, I would maintain their wedding night set these two young and sheltered people on a fateful path. And, their basic natures kept them to that path.

How could a cook presume to understand the nature of a prince? It came about first-hand, in a most unlikely fashion, that I had opportunity to take the measure of my future king.

In any kitchen there is always disappearance of supplies, but for a period, this theft became an epidemic. Meat and delicacies of the highest order were simply not there when First Cook needed to begin their preparation. He was at wit's end for any practical remedy and at last spoke to the King's steward about the problem.

To our amazement, the Dauphin, one day just appeared in the kitchen and began to ask us questions. My experience with courtiers was that most were arrogant and condescending. His manner was diffident and respectful, such that I would never have expected from a prince. He appeared again several days later with very practical locking devices that he had himself constructed. (16) Then he proceeded to install the devices on appropriate doors. When the locking devices worked, there was obvious relief among the workers that the cloud of suspicion over them had lifted, and he gained the admiration and respect of the entire staff.

It was then, by some intuition, I realized this shy young man would never be comfortable at court. He was a technician and a tinkerer. He had his workshop just as I had mine, and we both enjoyed what we produced. They were things that we could taste and touch, much different from the machinations at court.

In the days and weeks following the wedding, there was much to remind me of my assessments of the Prince and Princess. She was a stranger at the court and vulnerable. The function of any consort to royalty is to produce an heir. That the Princess was not fulfilling her role was obvious and did not endear her to her husband's family who were quick to seize upon her faults. It was not long before we heard accounts not only of her serious lack of education, but that she was barely able to read at all. Worst of all, it was her attitude that proved to be most harmful. Whether through ignorance, or youth and inexperience, the Princess was blithely unaware of all the currents at court. She was indeed like a doll playing at being princess.

The unassuming Prince was indulgent to his bride. It was not his nature to be forceful, but also there was probably some guilt, for he knew better than anyone why there was no heir.

In time the Princess established her domain in the Petit Trianon, a lovely small palace on the grounds of Versailles. Here, with a small clique of intimates, the Princess set the standards: no serious discussion was tolerated; everything frivolous and amusing was encouraged so that those surrounding her became a circle of unreality with no thought given to her future role as queen.

Four years later in 1774, the Princess at nineteen and the Dauphin at twenty, became the Queen and King of France. By now I was chief cook at Versailles. I saw to it that the kitchen staff for which I was responsible, outdid itself during the festivities of the coronation. Even so, it crossed my mind more than once that the Princess had done nothing to earn the affection of the people, and the Dauphin was reluctant to be King. These two assumed the throne while France was in a state of turmoil that begged for informed and compassionate involvement, and guidance that was firm. I wondered how these two would cope.

The country was distracted for a time when the Queen, after seven years of marriage, did come to be with child. That a disappointing girl was born did not improve the status of the Queen. The birth of the first Dauphin four years later helped, but spawned another set of problems. There were serious rumors afoot that the King was not father to either child.

Worse, I heard on good authority that such rumors were encouraged by the King's two brothers, each who thought he would make a better king. There was also a sister, Elizabeth, and two maiden aunts who had some degree of influence at court. All of them had their coterie of followers who pursued their own politics for their separate causes. Elizabeth however, did later prove devotion to the King and Queen by accompanying them through all their travails.

There are of course such politics at every court. Had King Louis been harsher or more worldly, there may have been less strife. But he was neither. He liked his workshop that was much less threatening than the undercurrents at court.

The first son born to King Louis and the Queen, Louis Xavier, displaced the King's brothers in succession to the throne. Whatever they could do to cast doubts on the first Dauphin's parentage, they did not hesitate to do. It was quite by accident and long after the rumors had subsided, that I learned for certain the King was father to his children despite the ugly stories.

A valet to the King , somewhat in his cups, stumbled into my kitchen at Versailles where I was in place to listen and offer solace. The valet confided information he should not have told …that early in his marriage, the King could not have conjugal relations due to a deformed ligament that required surgery to correct.

My sympathies were immediately with the King. Surgery of any kind was a fearful prospect…much more so in such a sensitive area. There was nothing to dull the pain, and death through surgery was more common than not. It was not surprising that the King procrastinated until an uncle persuaded him that the operation was essential to the preservation of the monarchy. With more courage than I would have had, the King did agree after delaying for seven years. So I learned the King was father to his children. Though I was privy to the truth through the valet, I was relieved the man did not keep his post for long. Even a king should be allowed to have some private secrets.

Two more children were born: Louis Charles four years after the first Dauphin and then a girl who did not live a year. However the Queen had conducted herself before she became a mother, all accounts were that she was maternal toward her children and became more responsible as Queen. But this was after a span of ten years or more during which her reputation had suffered. Such harm is not easily undone. With the help of her enemies at court, Marie Antoinette remained a foreigner and even was called a traitor when she was suspected of conspiring with her Austrian brother against France.

During our last years at Versailles, nothing in France seemed to improve. Whatever the King tried to do for reform was not enough or too late in coming. However the Queen matured in her role was not enough. Even Nature seemed to conspire against France as there were poor crops year after year.

The King and Queen received some favor and sympathy at the deaths of the first Dauphin and the infant girl, but this sympathy was fleeting. I came to believe that any mortal man faced with such overwhelming problems would find it a difficult road to try to solve them. These two especially, were ill-equipped for the roles Destiny had assigned to them. They were an unfortunate couple too easy to blame.

When the royal family was forced to move to the Tuileries in Paris, I followed. I no longer had ties or commitments at Versailles. My own good wife had recently died, and my two sons were seeking their fortunes elsewhere…one in America and one in England. At the Tuileries, I was again First Cook and encouraged my kitchen to be the center.

Gerard Gascon and Henri Pardeau, two Guardsmen to the royal family, and many others as well found their way to the kitchen. These two young men especially reminded me of my sons. They would often tell of experiences with their charges. Gerard was quite fond of Louis Charles, the little boy who was now the Dauphin. When the royal family escaped for those five days, I put on a stern face, but in my heart I wished they had escaped. In that last horrible uprising in the Tuileries, I will add that it was I who hid Henri in the cooking pot while I hid in the root cellar among onions and turnips.

***

These past pages are but a brief account of some events in which I played a part. They are only one man's observations and perceptions, though perhaps with some degree of merit. But I was also at The Temple throughout everything which I am about to relate: the imprisonment and execution of the King and Queen, and the tragic fate of the children. They are the events that are the heart of my story. And so I find myself here at The Temple still following my King, but appalled at his present condition, and the circumstances that brought him to this place. The Tuileries had been old and shabby, but livable. The Temple was another matter.

The Temple, where the royal family of France spent the last years of their lives.

The Temple had its origins with the very beginnings of Paris itself in the 12th century. An order of knights built it as a castle, but it also served as church. It had one large center tower surrounded by four smaller towers, and therefore sometimes called "The Tower". Most commonly it was known as "The Temple" and was a Paris landmark for centuries. The castle was as strong and fortified as any structure could be. That The Temple was selected to house the King and his family was significant.

It was the rare person in Paris and indeed in all of France who was not torn between the forces of the revolution. In my kitchen in the Tuileries on any given day, I could hear heated arguments either for tolerance and compromise or for total revolution. At times it was almost impossible to keep the peace enough to do the work. In my mind it became quite clear that those who supported drastic changes were gaining in numbers and in vehemence. Such ideas were being fueled by agitators who seemed to have no regard for consequences. When The Temple was selected, I took it as a surety that moderation was losing ground. Before long my reasoning proved itself.

The National Assembly reflected this conflict. If a person was in authority one day, someone else could be in place the next so that few decisions were final. So it was with arrangements for the King's imprisonment.

The Assembly decreed an allowance for the maintenance of the prisoners, but it was seldom dispensed. Very little attention was given to furnishings, comfort, or even basic needs, so that for a time, the family had not a change of linen or outer garments, and their chambers were not furnished. No expense was spared however, in securing their captivity: windows were walled in, trees were removed, outer walls were raised, and a moat was begun, and then for whatever unexplained reason, filled in again.

The family was under control of Paris officials called municipals who took their orders from the fickle Assembly. Any municipal on any whim or curiosity could, and did, intrude into the private quarters. Many of them did so on any pretext or simply to harass. Once the King for no sensible reason was roused from his bed. While he was in his nightshirt, he and his chamber were searched for weapons.

When the family was permitted exercise, they walked past guards and municipals who made rude remarks, blew smoke deliberately in their faces, or spat at their feet. A few guards and municipals were compassionate, but for most the urge to humiliate and demean their prisoners came easily.

Through all the insults and abuse, the King and Queen maintained a dignity and composure that drew admiration except from the cruelest. During conversations in the kitchen, I often overheard acknowledgment of the King's forbearance, grudging though it was, even from those who were unsympathetic. There was also grudging acknowledgment of the family's devotion to one another. In these most difficult of circumstances, they seemed to gain strength from this loyalty to each other.

Devoted attendants and friends were permitted to stay with the family at The Temple at first. Among them was Madame de Lamballe, in whose dreadful end I was soon to play a most unwelcome part. For several days there were fourteen who comprised the group within The Temple. But one evening, with no warning, this decision was reversed. Eight attendants, Lamballe among them, were taken away with no explanation. Only Hue, valet to the King, was permitted to return. Six others were imprisoned, interrogated, and were eventually released. Madame de Lamballe was not released.

When the King inquired as to their whereabouts, he was told only that they would not be returning, and that other officials would be assigned to assist the family. The King refused this offer of strangers who would intrude into their lives. Despite the King's objections, officials were imposed to the extent that they were always present.

In the last few months of his life, this unassuming man who was miscast into life at court with all its servitors, had with him only this wife, Marie Antoinette; his loyal sister, Elizabeth; his fifteen year old daughter, Teresa; his seven year old son, Louis Charles; and one attendant, his valet, Hue. Yet somehow he seemed more regal in this forbidding place than amidst all the ostentation at Versailles.

The King took pleasure in the lessons he gave to young Charles in French, Latin, history, geography, and arithmetic. The arithmetic was discontinued when a municipal interfered. He accused the King of using the child's arithmetic as code.

There were books left in The Temple so at least the family had reading as entertainment and diversion. But no news of the outside world was allowed to this man who was involved for many years with the affairs of his country and its people. In this respect, I was able to do some service.

I often went about the city for provisions for the kitchen, and in so doing collected news as well as papers and journals. The valet was the only one permitted to have direct contact with the family. Hue and I concocted a plan whereby someone distracted the ever present municipals, while I passed news material from the streets to him.

However, what we learned about the bloody September Massacres reached us much more directly through the death of the Princess de Lamballe, and in a most repulsive way, through me.

I had known of the Princess de Lamballe since our days at Versailles. When her death was so violently thrust upon me, I resolved to learn what I could to better understand such hatred as was directed against her.

Madame de Lamballe was friend to the Queen from Marie Antoinette's first days in France. The two princesses were bosom companions during the youthful nonsense at Petit Trianon and even after Marie became Queen and mother. Madame de Lamballe was Superintendent of the Queen's Household for a time at Tuileries, but she left France, as did many nobility when they felt the winds of change blowing against them. Any French noble who lived outside the country was called an 'émigré'. Many of them worked against the revolution and worked to preserve the monarchy; some for King Louis and some for his brothers. All émigrés were therefore suspect.

Whatever her politics, Madame de Lamballe was persuaded to return to France as an example to other émigrés. She joined the Queen at Tuileries and followed her to The Temple. When the officials reversed themselves on the number of attendants they would allow, Madame was taken to prison with the other seven, but she was not released with them. She died.

Two facts about her death are known…that she died on 3 September 1792, and what happened to her body. All else is a mystery.

When she entered prison, her name in the ledger was written larger as if for special attention. If she were to get special attention, there is no evidence of it. There are conflicting stories as to whether or not she was questioned at all. If she were not questioned, why was she not released? Some say her death was an official execution, but there is no record of a trial to justify an execution.

My nagging fear is that in the confusion of those days, Madame de Lamballe was a monumental oversight. She remained in prison because someone was negligent, or his orders were mislaid or misunderstood. Thus during the September Massacres, she became just one of those hapless prison victims…that is, until her body was recognized.

Whether executed or murdered, Madame's death should have been payment enough for any crime. It was not. As an added dishonor, her head, limbs, and even inner organs were dismembered and tossed out to the crowd who caught the body parts and added to the savagery by parading them. .

There was blood lust in the air…cries and oaths and threats and two names being screamed again and again, "La Lamballe!" and "The Austrian!" All of it was madness, but with a crazed direction … to The Temple to show the Queen what happened to her friend.

One man was not sure the Queen would recognize the bloody head with the disordered hair. He stopped at a salon where the hairdresser was forced to rearrange and fashion Madame Lamballes's hair on the head without a body. This horror I learned later. My direct part was soon to come.

In the kitchen of The Temple, I could hear the mob approach. Suddenly, the door burst open with a crash, and I was confronted by a man whose eyes were fiery red and frantic, and his face contorted with fury. In one hand he had what looked like bloody meat. A thousand times or more I wished I did not know the truth. It was the heart of Madame de Lamballe. The demented cannibal demanded that I cook the heart for he was hungry.

In my state of horror and revulsion, I doubt I could have acted in any way, but the creature was easily distracted by the frenzy outside. He left just as abruptly as he had entered, and I was spared. This memory comes more often to my mind than I would want. Each time I question that such behavior could be human. Then I remember that it was a fellow man, and I am ashamed.

When I recovered my senses, I ran to warn Hue to keep the family in the inner parts away from windows. I came too late. On the threat of allowing the mob to enter The Temple, a group of officials cruelly forced the Queen to the window. There, speared on a long pike, was the recognizable head of her friend, Madame de Lamballe. The Queen fainted.

***

The Massacres of September were a prelude to the terrors that were yet to come. The usual form of execution in France was beheading the culprit with an ax. As a cook, I knew that the cutting blade hits its mark only after much experience. An unwelcome thought intrudes. How does an executioner gain experience? I am forced to say, very like a butcher on meat...with practice. An executioner then, early in his trade (or later if his work is mediocre) could often miss his mark and need more than one blow of the ax or, miss his mark and so cut off limbs. Death should be enough punishment for even the worst offenders, without such additional suffering. A member of the National Assembly, Joseph Ignace Guillotin, was a doctor and was sympathetic to the problems of beheading with an ax. In pursuit of a humane remedy, he devised a machine which became known in his honor as the guillotine.

It was a rectangle frame made of sturdy wood that stood perhaps fifteen feet at its height. Between the standing wooden posts at the top was suspended a very heavy, sharpened, metal blade. At the base of the posts was the block that held the victim's head. When the blade was released from that height, it fell with great force to do the work intended. It was used in public for the first time the year before the King was executed. Very soon it became a most efficient killing machine, just in time for the worst phase of the revolution.

The National Assembly was re-forming and calling itself the Convention. Dominating these changes were the most radical of the revolutionaries. As I went about the streets of Paris, I could always find writings or hear agitators. They roused and stirred the people, not to their better natures, but to their worst. Violence and destruction were encouraged; kindness and compassion more and more were considered to be weaknesses.

The guillotine, invented by a doctor to be a more humane killing machine.

In this malignant atmosphere, the King and Queen bore the brunt of hatred. It was not enough that they were daily humiliated, always confined, and deprived of any power. Each new set of officials seemed duty-bound to impose another cruelty or humiliation: searches were increased to any hour of day or night;

books were taken apart to be inspected for hidden codes; table knives and forks were removed, and then allowed again, but only for meals; all pens and paper were confiscated, none even for the lessons of the children. For the women, a major diversion as well as necessity was mending their clothes, until the scissors and needles were taken from them.

The entire family, including the King and Hue, became ill with fever. I was permitted to tend Hue for one night, but the Queen was not given the same privilege for the care of her son.

The adults were quite aware this downward spiral of abuses could have only one end…execution. But most difficult for the prisoners was the torture of uncertainty. Officials took actions with no explanation and greatly increased the anxiety for the family. They never knew what day could be the last. I witnessed the evils of it all and marveled at their endurance.

At last on December 11, 1792, municipals came for the King to bring him before the Convention. In the usual muddled, heartless manner, they came in the morning while the Dauphin was at his lessons with the King. Quite rudely, their first action was to remove young Charles to his mother's chamber. For three more hours there was delay with officials milling about and no further action taken. We later learned it was because some incompetent had neglected to bring along the decree authorized by the Convention.

Everything waited. Deprived of any worthwhile activity, the King sat and made no movement for some time. At this, an official approached. The King asked the man, *"What do you want of me?"*

The man replied, *"I was afraid that you were ill."*

"No; I am obliged to you, but the manner in which they have deprived me of my son has deeply afflicted me." (17) At last at one o'clock, the mayor of Paris came with the decree to escort the King to the carriage which was to carry him to trial. An elaborate escort was provided. There were spectators along the route, but they were subdued. The people seemed to realize a King was being taken to trial, and that it was a solemn occasion.

The King had been brought before the Convention prematurely. Charges against him were incomplete and still being compiled. Officials did allow the King to make arrangements to obtain counsel for his defense. The King was then returned to The Temple, but was ordered to have no communication of any kind with his family... more cruelty.

Again Hue and I conspired to defy these orders by any means we could devise. When a note needed to be delivered, I would wrap the note inside a ball of bread and throw the ball where Hue would be sure to find it. Hue saved string to make a message carrier between the King's chamber and his sister's. In these silly ways, we helped the family maintain contact so that the uncertainty of no information at all did not defeat their spirits.

The King had, for months during his imprisonment, been interpreting the unfavorable signs of his treatment. Except for a very few individuals on rare occasions, there was nothing to indicate that he would receive fairness or mercy. In his own mind, with or without a trial, he was already resigned to the inevitable outcome. He had come to terms with his own death. In so doing, he found peace. This inner peace was reflected in his dealings with all those around him: his family, a few loyal servants, his guards and tormentors, and even his judges. He had an aura of composure and tranquility. Thus, whoever came near him in those last days was witness to his truest nobility.

Hue and I, between ourselves, determined that I should attend the trial, since he could be more useful to the family. I was to go and then provide an account of the proceedings to Hue which he would then relay to the Queen any way he could.

The King was ordered to appear on the day after Christmas. I followed after him as soon as I possibly could. Appropriately, it was a gloomy, rainy, windy, wintry day, and yet the streets were thronged with people. Again this day, the people were reserved as the King's carriage and a cavalry escort passed by.

Since it was my responsibility to observe in the interests of the Queen, I did not hesitate to use my elbows to gain admittance to the Convention. I had expected that this would be a daily exercise; that in such a serious matter, there would be lengthy proceedings. Instead it was a farce, and over in one day.

The King had three counsels who aided him in the preparation of his defense. Only one of them, Del`eze, spoke to the Convention. He presented the arguments for the defense logically, forcefully, and with great dignity for three hours. The Convention listened attentively and even responded favorably to some points in the defense. I thought I sensed a thoughtful hush when Del`eze confronted the Convention with these words: regarding the trial:

"...its importance, its solemnity, its brilliancy, its re-echo in future ages, would have merited months of meditation and effort, but for which (I) had only been allowed eight days...I seek among you judges, and I see among you only accusers!" (20)

The King spoke briefly but with poignancy: *"Gentlemen, my defence has been laid before you...In speaking to you, perhaps for the last time, I declare to you that my conscience bears me no reproach, and that my counsel have only told you the truth. I have never feared to have my conduct publicly investigated; but my heart is deeply pained at finding in the indictment, the imputation that I wished to shed the blood of the people."* (21) A few more words from the King, and it was done.

Del`eze was correct. The members of the Convention were not impartial judges. No sooner did the King and his counsels leave, but the enemies of the King renewed with vengeance their arguments against him. But to execute a king is among the worst of crimes. There were those in the Convention and among the people who were reluctant to take such a drastic measure as regicide. The debate continued into the new year.

Finally on the 17th of January in 1793, the vote was taken. The King was condemned to death at the guillotine. The decision was especially repugnant when we learned the majority voting for his death was only by five votes. In games and legislation, winning by five is acceptable. In matters of life and death, such a tiny majority is a heinous injustice.

The date for the execution of the King was set for 21st January, only four days hence and with good reason. Haste was essential so as not to give opponents of regicide time to gather forces. During those four days, serious precautions were taken to prevent rescue or suicide.

On this last day, there were preparations everywhere along the route from The Temple to the Place de la Revolution. The primary consideration was prevention of any escape, even death by an assassin. Informers were dispersed among the people. Drummers were placed along the route to help drown sounds of demonstration. All windows and doors were ordered to be closed. Every military force was ordered to duty. The avengers of the revolution were taking extraordinary measures to make sure the execution remained the righteous cause they had proclaimed that it was.

The practice of his religion had always been important to the King. Now especially he needed the comfort of the Sacraments to prepare himself for eternity. Even at this extremity, it seemed possible that the King would be denied Communion. Officials feared the wine brought by the priest could be the means for suicide.

The night before he died, the King asked to see his family. His wife, children and sister were brought to him in the evening. They were allowed to be alone together, but in a room with windows so that they were always under observation. Their words were mercifully private except for Teresa's account. *"My father at the moment he was leaving us for ever made us promise never to think of avenging his death."* (22)

There were many embraces and tears during those two hours. Emotions as they parted were heart-rending. Afterwards, the King spent the remainder of his last night with his Confessor and did receive Communion.

The fateful day, the 21st did not dawn. It merely lightened with an icy fog of gloom. Trumpets and drums awakened the people to announce it was no ordinary day. I could not bring myself to attend the execution. I did not want to see or hear the scene. There were memories enough to haunt my dreams. I do not wish to dwell on any part except to say the King, as I had come to expect, conducted himself with courage, strength, and dignity. At twenty-two minutes past ten in the morning, the efficient guillotine did its work. The severed head was lifted by the executioner for all to see.

Later I found words from a historian, de Beauchesne, that express my own thoughts very well. *"Destined by Heaven to be a martyr, Louis XVI had not the heroic energy to resist, but he had the heroic courage which knows how to die."* (23) He died as he had lived…a human being with virtues and faults, but to the end, a King.

***

Somewhere in my life I had heard of the story of Hercules and the Hydra. The Hydra was a nine-headed serpent. It could not be killed in usual ways, because each time a head was cut, two heads grew back.

There were enemies everywhere. Outside France it was the war with Austria, and other monarchies who were appalled at regicide. Inside the country, any who dared to question the road the revolution was taking, were branded as enemies and persecuted.

The new government of the Convention took action to eliminate enemies by appointing two committees: The Committee for General Security and the Committee for Public Safety. The Committee for Public Safety grew more powerful than the Convention itself for one reason…Robespierre was the key figure. He and his cronies influenced every decision of the government. Spies were everywhere. Neighbors were encouraged to testify against neighbors. Patrols searched any home, day or night, with a warrant only from the Committee. No dissent was tolerated.

These two committees set out to slay the Hydra of opposition. Their weapon was the blade of the guillotine. Yet, for every head cut off, others grew back in its place. The bloodshed seemed to be endless. In some parts of France, the guillotine was too slow. In one place, three hundred were killed with canon shot, while in another, two thousand were tied together in pairs and drowned in the river. One would think in such an atmosphere, the existence of one little boy would be overlooked. But no.

Charles, who was imprisoned in the Temple, was still a threat to the revolution. Immediately at the death of King Louis, the Count de Provence, the King's brother (an émigré living in Westphalia) declared young Charles to be King Louis XVII. Since the new king was only eight years old, the Count also declared himself to be regent for the boy. The monarchy was powerless, but it was not dead. It was another Hydra.

I kept my post as chief cook at The Temple, but with Hue no longer in service to the King, I was at a disadvantage. I had no excuse for direct contact with the remaining family. Neither was it safe nor wise to show them any sympathy. But I had nurtured an assistant cook, by name Caron, whose loyalty I had earned. I made him server to the family. In this way through his observations, I managed to keep informed. However, I could find no way to pass information to them. They did not know that Charles was declared to be the new king, except that it was his heritage.

Their keepers however, were on guard that no special attention be given the boy. Caron told me that the keepers made the Queen remove a cushion on which Charles was seated in a low chair for his dinner. They saw the cushion as an elevation paying some kind of homage to his rank. But this was a small annoyance, and no measure of what was to come.

Suspicion, fear, rumors, and lies were rampant. Especially troubling were the many rumors of plots brewing supposedly to bring Louis XVII to official power. They were the ones most threatening to the revolution and in this way proved to be most harmful to young Charles. With no investigation to prove whether or not there were such plots, the Committee of Public Safety decreed that the son of Louis Capet should be separated from his mother, and that a tutor would be assigned to the boy to allow better surveillance. No thought or consideration was given to the fears of a child. The decree was quickly signed. The last ordeal for Louis Charles had begun, and I was helpless to do anything except try to provide an honest account

They came as if they feared the day. At ten o'clock on the evening on 7 July, while the women were sewing and Charles was sleeping, six municipals arrived. They came to remove Charles from his mother. Her actions were no longer those of Marie Antoinette the Queen. She acted now only as a mother. The mother used every argument, gave excuses to delay, pleaded to keep her child. Her son was young. He needed her. The boy was ill. Just a few more days till he was better. Do you not have children of your own? The proud woman wept before these officials, uselessly. Their response was if she did not allow the boy to go peacefully, they would take him by force. By these threats, the mother gave up her child. Louis Charles, already an orphan once, was taken from his bed and from his mother to the Tower to the very rooms which his father had occupied. He was put under the care of Simon, a cobbler by trade.

That a crude, uneducated man was given the title of "tutor" to Charles, an intelligent, innocent child of privilege was debasing in itself. Worse, what contributed greatly to the tragedy to come, was that Simon was also the product of hatred spewed by Marat and Robespierre .

From their earliest public days, Marat and Robespierre knew of Simon. He went to their gatherings and was useful to their cause. Simon was a willing follower; a flunky who did as he was told, supported their ideas, and did not question their methods. In their distorted view, Simon was a revolutionary patriot whose name came to mind when a keeper was necessary for the son of King Louis XVI.

Simon did on rare occasions visit my kitchen, but never for long. Just enough that I could take measure of him. He once complained that his orders were that he or his wife must be on constant duty with the brat. On the other hand there were compensations of food, lodging, and money. Now that the brat was "learning his place," the work wasn't hard either. On another visit, when he was somewhat tipsy with a looser tongue, it seemed to weigh on his mind that the orders he received for the boy were too vague. Simon seemed unsure of his ground. He told me (with the kind of boasting that comes from an underling who confronts authority) that he demanded of the Committee, "*What do you want done with him? Do you want him transported? Killed? Poisoned?*" To all of these, the answer from the officials was, "*No.*"

When Simon asked, "*But what, then?*" the answer was, "*We want to be rid of him!*" (24)

Though the answer was still vague, Simon took it that his methods would not be questioned. In this assumption, he was correct. All of us in The Temple came to understand that Simon had authority over the boy, and that he had the support of the Committee of Public Safety. Even a doctor, those few times that one was brought, could not dispute Simon's treatment of the boy.

During his first few days in the Tower, Charles refused to eat in spite of threats from Simon. Caron reported that once he heard the boy confront Simon with great spirit to demand, "*I wish to know what law it is by which you are ordered to separate me from my mother and keep me in prison. Show me the law, I wish to see it!*" (25) Imagine! This kind of courage from a child, alone, and defying his jailer!

At other times the boy refused to speak at all and stood or sat unmoving and dejected. These small instances of resistance were not seen by Simon as unhappiness at separation from his mother. They were seen as rebellion and defiant pride from this boy who, though defenseless, still acted like royalty. To Simon such behavior would not be tolerated. The "wolf cub" as Simon called him, had to be made to understand that he no longer had privilege or status in the new order. Simon the 'tutor' proceeded to 'teach' the child about the new reality. At one time or another, Caron reported these incidents to me:

- The Queen sent lesson books and papers to Charles. Simon used them to light his pipe. As a result, there was nothing to occupy the child's mind or to divert his attention.

- Charles had arrived at the Tower with a suit suitable for mourning his father. The suit was discarded. A coat of red, a revolutionary color, was made for the boy. Marat had just been murdered. Simon forced the jacket on the boy to honor Marat.

- Songs and poems about regicide were heard all over Paris. Simon brought these from the streets and made the boy recite them even though they were a cruel reminder of his father's death.

- Charles was given the most menial household chores including polishing the shoes of Simon and his wife. He also had to kneel and wash their feet.

- As a gesture of power intended to demean, Simon had the long, chestnut curls that were Charles' shining glory, shorn.

Louis Charles, before his long hair was cut by Simon the cobbler.

Since the two keepers were obligated to stay with the boy, they were confined, also. This began to have its effect particularly on Simon. His drinking increased. In his cups, he became even more abusive using oaths, vile language, slaps and pushes and kicks with his orders to the boy. But worse, he forced the boy to eat to the point of gluttony and to drink wine till Charles was drunk.

His methods were successful. These 'lessons' from Simon were so effective that Charles became a cowering, dejected, unresponsive shell of the charming boy he had been only three months before. The boy's spirit was defeated. Now he could be used to their purpose… to testify against his mother.

Marie Antoinette was able to see her son only twice during this time even though they were both in The Temple. These were merely glimpses of her child through slits in a thick wall that separated them.

Charles' only exercise was an occasional walk with Simon as his guard. These walks came about at Simon's convenience at irregular times. The mother saw her son after hours of waiting at the slits day after day. Perhaps it would have been better if she had not seen for herself.

At the first sighting, she heard Simon's oaths and saw his mistreatment as Charles stumbled with bowed head to avoid Simon's blows. The second time, her son wore the colors of the revolution, and his beautiful hair was cut. The Queen had gotten some reports about her son from a sympathetic guard. To spare her, the guard had told only a partial story. After she saw her son abused and forlorn, she wept, "*I care for nothing now…I am too miserable not to dread some misfortune is approaching. My child! My child! I feel by the anguish of my own heart that his is failing him.*" (26)The Queen was correct in both her assumptions: more misfortune was coming, and her son's heart was weakening.

Again away from the light of day, this time at two o'clock in the morning on the 1st of August, municipals came for the Widow

Capet, as the Queen was called after Louis was executed. Under the ruling of the Tribunal Extraordinary, she was also to be separated from her daughter and sister-in-law until her trial.

That the Tribunal was planning a trial at all was a sop to the public. There was some flimsy evidence of plots in support of royalty by England and other countries in anonymous letters. These letters produced inflammatory oratory in the Convention about the plots, and the Widow Capet was often mentioned in the harangues against monarchy. As the trial date approached, no evidence was found, and no letters of conspiracy were produced. The trial was staged to justify what had already been decided. Marie Antoinette's fate was sealed long ago That there was no evidence against her presented a temporary problem that the officials solved with no restraint of conscience.

They attacked her on many counts as a wife and as a mother. Among these charges, was that as a wife, her behavior was wicked and immoral, and that she participated in shameful orgies. As a mother, it was worse. The charges against her were of depraved debaucheries, and that she had involved her children in these heinous acts. All the charges against her were written in a deposition,

The Committee of Public Safety understood that without witnesses, the case against the former queen might not bring the results they desired. Witnesses were necessary. The Committee visited the Tower where Simon was waiting with Marie Antoinette's son.

At first Charles resisted the insults about his mother from Simon even after he was beaten. But he was after all a little boy. By the time the Committee members came to the Tower with the deposition ready to be signed, the child was weakened. Whether from fatigue, or wine, or hopelessness, or simply the number of adult bodies aligned against one small boy, Charles signed the malicious deposition. The officials had their witness.

Elizabeth and Teresa were also questioned, but separately. Each was terrified when the other was taken, not knowing if either would return as the King and Queen and Charles had not returned. Elizabeth and Teresa denied the accusations in the deposition, but their denials were meaningless to the Committee for Public Safety. All three depositions were presented at the trial. There were witnesses for and against the defense, but the trial was over in one day. The most memorable words were those spoken by the Queen when she was asked if she wished to speak in her own defense:

"Nothing in my own defence, but much for your remorse to feel. I was a queen, and you dethroned me; I was a wife, and you murdered my husband; a mother, and you have torn my children from me: I have nothing left but my blood, ~ take it then; hasten to shed it, that you may quench your thirst therewith." (27)

Marie Antoinette in a cart going to execution.

Back in her cell, she readied herself for what was to come. She wrote a letter to her sister-in-law and asked that Elizabeth not think too harshly of what Charles had done. In the same letter she asked that Charles be reminded of his father's words to seek no revenge. She closed with the words, *"I forgive all my enemies the injuries they have done me."* (28) When her letter was done, a priest in disguise had somehow gained entry and was able to say a mass and give her the Sacrament.

On 16 October, nine months after her husband was executed, officials came for her at eleven o'clock in the morning. The Widow Capet, a citizen, was not taken to the scaffold in a carriage, but in a dirty, horse-drawn cart with a plank for her seat. She herself was dressed in white with a white cap trimmed with black ribbon around her cap and at her wrists. She was but thirty-eight years old, but the short hair showing under her cap was white. The last years since Versailles had taken their toll.

There were crowds of people along the route of the cart, but few demonstrations either in her behalf or against her. Her hands still bound behind her, she took the steps up to the guillotine alone. She refused assistance. Her last words were to the executioner, *"Make haste!"* (29)

Nor did I attend the execution of the Queen. I had had enough of bloodshed. All the circumstances leading her to the scaffold and to her death, I pieced together from many sources. It was as if I had appointed myself to be chronicler for this unfortunate family. If this were to be my role. I meant to do the work as best I could. For this I was well placed.

The kitchen was still my best source for information from guards and passing officials. Polite interest and courtesy were often enough to start a story, for there are few who can resist telling about the importance of the work they do.

There is one particular incident that occurred at The Temple that provides an insight into the times. It came to be known as the "Conspiracy of the Canaries" and deserves attention for its absurdity.

There was a servant who had worked himself into the good will of Simon. He was a kind man who understood the deprivation of young Charles. He resolved to help the boy and somehow received permission from Simon to give to Charles a mechanical canary which he found in the storeroom. The canary flapped its wings in its cage and also sang "The King's March," a song well-known before the revolution. The canary was the first amusement Charles had been given since he came under Simon's care. He was pleased with the toy for a time, but tired of it before long. That Charles had shown any interest, inspired the servant to bring a live canary whose antics were so entertaining to the boy that the servant collected perhaps ten more canaries all willingly donated as gifts for the Dauphin, as Charles was still known.

The birds were all tame and lively and warbling and cheered the dullness of the prison. One bird was especially responsive to Charles. The bird would sit on the boy's shoulder or his finger and eat from his hand. To distinguish his pet from the others, Charles tied a bit of pink ribbon to its leg.

This diversion from the canaries lasted only until the next visit from the officials. The men happened to arrive at the very time the mechanical bird was singing the "King's March." At the same time, the live pet bird was warbling, which made it appear the pet bird was singing royalist words.

One municipal was outraged. *"What is the meaning of that seditious song, and the pink ribbon adorning a privileged bird, like a decoration?"* (30)

The incident was reported to the Committee which immediately issued a prohibition against all birds, live or mechanical, within The Temple. Thus, the one diversion provided for Charles by a kind-hearted servant became a travesty of common sense. It could also be seen as an omen.

Shortly thereafter, Simon resigned. The Committee elected not to replace Simon. What happened next for the boy almost makes Simon seem to be kindly, though I am ashamed to allow such a thought to enter my mind. If nothing else is remembered from my accounts, it must be very clear that Simon was evil; that he was a tormentor, abuser, and cruel bully to a helpless child. I would hope that whatever status he keeps in history, I would contribute to his being remembered as an abomination.

Nevertheless, Simon did provide contact with people, however warped the contact was. The boy also received a measure of physical care, though it was erratic and interspersed with neglect or abuse.

Now, at the beginning of 1794, Charles was in total isolation. He was in one small room with bars and padlocks. There was a bed and blanket. He did have clothes, and food was brought. Whether or not Charles or his cell stayed clean depended on his own efforts. There was a kind of basket shelf on which to place food or supplies going into the room and on which Charles could place anything to go out. But there was no heat except for a stovepipe passing through his cell, no light, and no person to comfort or to speak to him. The only indication of anything human was the hand of Caron when it placed his food into the basket, and any voice that ordered the boy to bed.

At first, the boy did make efforts to keep himself and his room clean and tidy, but he was after all not quite nine years. I doubt that any grown man or woman could withstand such deprivation without losing either the inclination to keep up appearances or the heart to do so.

The world outside The Temple was aware that Louis Charles existed, but only a few, counted on one hand, knew under what conditions. Even these few had nothing but suspicions of how deplorable these conditions actually were. When the truth finally did become known, those of us closest were appalled at the horrors of the child's existence.

The Committee of Public Safety during this Jacobin terror continued its work. Any leaders who were so rash as to work for any kind of moderation were disposed of by imprisonment or the guillotine. In this seething cauldron, three members of the royal family remained, Teresa, her aunt Elizabeth, and Charles.

In early May at bedtime, they came for Elizabeth. "*Citizenness, come downstairs directly, thou art wanted.*" The aunt tried to reassure her young niece by telling her not to fear, "*Be composed, I shall come again!*" (31) But reality had schooled Teresa. She knew very well that those who were led away did not return. This time, Elizabeth also did not return.

In a mockery of a trial, before one judge, Elizabeth (with twenty-four others) was accused of conspiracy to restore the monarchy. There was no evidence or witnesses. One counsel tried to speak in her defense. He recalled that Elizabeth had chosen to stay with her brother and his family throughout their troubles. The counsel reminded the judges that her behavior was considered to be a model for virtues valued by Frenchmen. Instead, showing no sympathy, the judge took it upon himself to berate the counsel for "*corrupting public morality*" (32) with such a sentiment. In a matter of hours, Elizabeth and the twenty-four others were condemned.

Since there were so many waiting for the guillotine, a bench on which they could sit was considerately provided. As each person stood to mount the scaffold, each one bowed before Elizabeth. Among themselves and the spectators, there were those who valued the virtues of devotion and loyalty that Elizabeth had demonstrated to the very end.

Now Teresa, a princess of seventeen years of age who should have been attending her first ball, was also alone in prison.

The Revolution became a question of survival. Whatever warring force gained power, its first official act was to condemn the opposing force. It was a risk to offer any opinion aloud, so that certainly only those most hungry for leadership and power would obviously work to get it. The carnage continued. Leaders of factions simply destroyed each other so that there was continual opportunity for the ones fortunate enough to survive.

***

Earlier in my life, there were many occasions when I questioned whether or not there was any justice in the world. So many times it seemed good deeds were not rewarded, and evil was not punished. I can now say for a certainty that I know of two instances where life itself did mete out, in its own way, a kind of justice that was quite satisfying.

The first was Jean-Paul Marat, a spewer of words of hatred and violence. Charlotte Corday, a woman in an opposing group, took Marat's teachings to heart. She stabbed him while he was in his bath. The second was Robespierre who was to receive a kind of poetic justice. This man, this great proponent of the use of the guillotine was himself condemned to the guillotine. For this I needed to be a witness.

Robespierre was in the company of nineteen of his cohorts. They were all being transported in rude carts to the scaffold. As I was searching for the face of Robespierre, my heart gave a leap at the unexpected sight of Simon seated in the same tumbrel. Here, though I consider myself to be a compassionate man, for those two, I deliberately pushed down any sympathies I may have felt. Truthfully, I did not need to struggle much.

Simon's crimes to the Dauphin were not known to the public at that time. He was almost unnoticed, as were the others in the carts. As for Robespierre, it seemed that for every person he had had arrested or killed, there were two along the road to shout invective's at the passing tumbrel. They, and many others who knew his methods, made up throngs along the route. Robespierre's clothes were torn, dirty and splattered with blood. His jaw was bloody and appeared to be broken, and one eye was hanging on his cheek. Certainly he had been mistreated and probably tortured.

The crowd was unruly and boisterous, but I saw one man stand quietly as the cart with Simon and Robespierre passed. He spoke aloud the words that I was feeling. Solemnly, but in a tone of approval, he said, *"Here is proof. There is a God!"* I added a hearty *"Amen!"* (33)

We looked at each other with understanding, and then I walked away. I did not need to see the bloody act after all. It was enough that these two were on their way.

***

In my private reflections, I have often wondered how it was that other monarchies who had a vested interest in protecting royalty, did not make more efforts to rescue the royals of France. Many years later, the world learned there had been such attempts both serious and flimsy, besides the escape to Varennes. After the King was executed, there were also two serious attempts to rescue the remaining family from The Temple. Neither succeeded, once because a note was discovered and alerted Simon, and once Marie Antoinette herself, from fear, changed her mind at the eleventh hour. It is the "ifs" that make the tragedy of this family so intense…if, if, if, and every if is thwarted by a conscious choice made by some participant.

But the rescue attempts did have two effects. The first was that Charles was separated from his mother. Second, rumors are always rife when information is scarce. In the case of the prince being held captive in The Tower, they multiplied. Most kind people did not want to believe a child was left in isolation and in need. Therefore, many stories developed of his rescue and escape. He was seen somewhere in France, in England, in America, or in Canada. How much better for Charles had any of these rumors been true.

Rather, both children remained in The Temple. Each was alone, though conditions for Teresa were not so forbidding. Still, it was some time before she learned as fact that her mother and aunt were dead, though most likely her intuition assured her it was true.

In the months after her mother and aunt were removed, she saw Charles only once and that by accident. They were not allowed to exchange any words at all, only to look at each other in passing. This brief sight of her brother was enough that Teresa wrote letters on his behalf stating that he was ill. She asked that she be permitted to help care for him. She received no reply.

Those of us who knew the boy was in his cell, tried to learn of his health, but we could get no specific information. Even if we had, we still could have done nothing.

After Simon and Robespierre were executed, a new man, by name Laurent, was assigned by the revolutionary committee to oversee all matters in The Temple. Laurent at last, was a man with the courage to think and act for himself. His first official decision was to insist that he be allowed to examine the prisoner. That common sense request opened not only the rusted, padlocked door to Charles' cell to admit another human, it opened the door to a vault of horror.

It is particularly galling to me that even those few of us in The Temple who cared about the child, had no way to know the reality of what Charles had endured. There were groups of men who worked round the clock to guard the boy. How was it that not a one of them was troubled enough to look a little deeper? Perhaps it was simply the differences among men: some ignorant, some cruel, some going through the motions of doing work, some negligent, and most assuming the nature of jailers who guarded the body, but paid no heed to other needs. True, the locks on the door were rusted from disuse which would have made entry more difficult, Whatever the reasons, no one had entered the cell for six months. During those six months, whenever a new group came on duty day or night, they called to the body they were guarding and demanded a response to reassure themselves. Others more cruel, called to him for amusement. Such calls interrupted his sleep, yet sleep was the only way there was for Charles to ease the interminable hours.

Often it was just negligence. Sometimes food was delayed or forgotten altogether.

At no time was any effort made by anyone to provide fresh air. No windows were opened, and no arrangements were made for exercise of any kind; not for one hour a week or for one hour a month…none at all for those six months.

And worst of all, there was the isolation.

Through this accumulation of mistreatment, (and I include the six months previously with Simon) Charles became weak, debilitated, and consequently more lethargic as the weeks passed. He had to leave his bed to get his food and water from the basket. To his own detriment, sometimes he did not. He did not sweep or clean his room. He stopped washing himself. His clothes went to rags, and his sheets were in tatters. He did not think to turn his pallet or probably had not the strength, nor would it have made much difference if he had.

When Laurent and the other officials broke through the locks and forced open the door, they were assaulted by putrid odors of decay. Dust and dirt and filth were everywhere. Rats and mice had made nests in the room. As to the condition of the prisoner, that was enough to touch the cruelest heart.

Of course, we in The Temple heard very soon what Laurent discovered in the cell, but years later I found words better than I could describe, again by the historian de Beauchesne, that gave in great detail those actual conditions. I have the entirety in my possession, but will include here only the essentials.

"In a dark room, from which exhaled an odour of corruption and death, on a dirty unmade bed barely covered with a filthy cloth and ragged pair of trousers, a child of nine years old was lying motionless, his back bent, his face wan and wasted with misery…an expression of most mournful apathy…His head and neck were fretted by purulent sores; his legs, thighs, and arms were lengthened disproportionately; his knees and wrists were covered with blue and yellow swellings; his feet and hands… were armed with nails of immense length having the consistency of horn; on his little temples, the beautiful hair…given up to attacks of vermin, was stuck fast by an inveterate scurf like pitch; his body was also covered with vermin; bugs and lice crowded together in folds of his ragged sheets and blanket, over which great black spiders crawled." (34)

The officials who entered the cell spoke to the figure on the bed repeatedly, but there was no response until one of them asked why the boy did not eat his food. At last Charles replied, *"No, I want to die!"* (35)

Laurent, although he was a supporter of the revolution, demonstrated his humanity from the first. Even though there was considerable resistance from the other officials, Laurent persisted until he got warm water to tend at least the sores on the boy. He continued demanding until his charge was moved to another room into a clean bed, and a surgeon was assigned to care for the boy. A woman was found to bathe Charles and cut his hair. A new suit of clothes was ordered.

At first Charles was unresponsive. His head and body were very tender. As the sores were tended and his hair unsnarled, Charles suffered through these attentions, but sometimes cried out in pain. Then quite unexpectedly one day, he apologized to the surgeon and thanked him for his care.

Charles slowly improved enough so that Laurent thought it appropriate to take Charles for a walk on the wall of the Tower where there was at last fresh air, daylight, and sounds from the street below. But one most significant custom that Laurent started was to call the boy "Charles" or "Monsieur" or "Monsieur Charles" rather than by "Capet" or some other demeaning name. With such basic kindnesses, the boy became less fearful so that he would speak at times. Still, he shrank from strangers and would not speak to them.

Depending on who had influence in the Committee of Public Safety and in the Convention, it appeared at times that consideration was being given to possible release of the children. Then the Convention reverted, and everything was as usual. Laurent could get no further concessions for the children. He objected to the constraints put upon him and repeatedly requested for another person to share his responsibility.

Throughout the next year, there were several others who were assigned to The Temple. One was Gomin who was recommended to the job by a royalist who pretended to be a republican. In quiet ways Gomin was able to aid both Charles and his sister.

As always with strangers, Charles did not respond to Gomin for some weeks even though Gomin was thoughtful in many ways to the boy. When he learned Charles liked flowers, he brought a pot of blossoms one day as a gift. The boy's eyes brightened at the cheerful gift, but he did not speak. Weeks later as Gomin became more familiar to him, Charles remembered the flowers and thanked Gomin in words.

Charles did improve in appearance and strength for a time, but the improvement was temporary. Some days he was too pained to walk at all. Gomin tended him as best he could and continued to show him small attentions until he won the boy's confidence. One day when they were entirely alone, Charles pleaded with Gomin, "*I want to see her one once more, let me see her before I die, I beseech you!*" (36)

Gomin was shaken. At first he assumed that Charles was asking to see his sister. Even that was not possible to accomplish. But then he realized that Charles was pleading to see his mother. The boy did not know his mother was dead. What bitterness he must have felt toward his jailers who were keeping him from the mother he thought was still in The Temple. Neither did he see his sister again, though their rooms were steps apart.

The months without air and exercise and proper food had a profound effect on his growing-child's body. As a result, his body was rickety and his legs were distorted and weak. The superficial sores had healed, but he had several abscesses on his body that were due to scrofula, a serious disease. As the months passed, his condition worsened.

Laurent, who was the first to bring light to that Tower room, resigned his post. I was sorry to see him go, not knowing what authority would take his place that might undo the good that had been done for the boy. But the new director for The Temple, Lasne by name, was also a kindly man. Lasne and Gomin formed an alliance that worked very well to ease the last days of Charles.

Both men alternated their care of Charles, but in concert. Each knew what the other did and agreed to it. They were both attentive and thoughtful and willing to take time to play simple games. They brought trinkets for his amusement, took him for walks and carried Charles if necessary. They made music...Gomin with the violin and Lasne singing, which pleased Charles very much even though the music was more hearty than skillful. But the best part for Charles was that Lasne, a former Guardsmen, remembered the boy from the Tuileries, a happier time when the boy was surrounded by his family. Charles especially liked to hear that Lasne remembered him in his uniform, drilling with his little musket or his sword.

The disease continued to advance. In early May 1795, both Lasne and Gomin were so concerned about his health that they thought it wise to inform the authorities. There was no response for a week or more, and then an elderly physician was sent. He prescribed country air. This recommendation of course was ignored. The doctor tended Charles only for five days when he himself died. I mention him because his death contributed greatly to all the varied stories about the death of the Dauphin.

Gomin or Lasne was always with the boy during the day as were physicians who came and went. But even in these dire circumstances, the child was alone with his pain at night...until the last night of 7 July. Both men must have sensed the end was near. They alternated staying with Charles through the night. As Lasne left, Gomin stayed. He sat down near the boy's bed for some time, but did not speak so as not to disturb Charles.

When Charles stirred, Gomin asked, *"I hope you are not in pain, just now?"*

"Oh! Yes! I am still in pain, but not nearly so much ~ the music is so beautiful!"

Since there was no music to be heard, Gomin asked, *"From what direction do you hear the music?"*

"From above...Do you not hear it? Listen! Listen! And then according to Gomin's account, a peaceful, happy expression settled on the boy's face, when he cried out, *"From amongst all the voices, I have distinguished that of my mother!"*

Gomin sat holding the child's hand until Lasne came. He too sat quietly beside the bed, when Charles spoke, "*Do you think my sister could have heard the music? How much good it would have done her!*" And a little later, *"I have something to tell you!"*(37)

Lasne leaned close to hear, but there were no other words. Charles breathed his last breath at two o'clock in the morning of 8 July 1795. He was ten years old.

***

Through all the comings and goings to and from The Temple, word of the serious illness of the Dauphin did seep to the outside world. On hearing this one way or another, the people began to collect. There were many who had not forgotten their little prince. They gathered with foreboding, but in sympathy and affection. None of us learned of his death for two days. To the officials, the death of Charles was an inconvenience.

When Gomin came to them with the news, the National Convention was not in session. They ordered Gomin to keep the secret until a committee could meet. This delay, and several other errors in judgment, helped to cause unnecessary confusion and suspicions later.

The next day, committee members and various guardsmen who had seen the boy at Tuileries and at The Temple, were gathered. They were asked to attest to this being the body of the son of Louis XVI and Marie Antoinette. There were at least ten men who had known the boy and gave witness that the body was the same as the boy they had known previously. History may have been satisfied if this had been the only group, but there were others who added to the confusion. Surgeons were designated to dissect the body to determine the cause of death. After the surgeons completed their work, another new group of officials arrived to prepare the body for burial. These different sets of people added greatly to all the suspicions and rumors surrounding the death of the Dauphin.

The last officials went up to the Tower where the body was lying naked and uncovered on a wooden plank. A coffin was produced, and the body was laid inside when one young official took his handkerchief and placed it under the head. At this simple act of respect, another man found a sheet. There were no shoes or stockings, no costly suit, no jewelry; nothing to signify that Charles was a prince…only the sheet that served as a shroud. The body was placed in an unadorned pine coffin, the lid was nailed shut, the coffin was placed on a litter carried to the courtyard, and then covered with a black cloth.

It was seven o'clock in the evening… still daylight on one of the longest days of the year. Some citizens were already gathered at The Temple. The coffin was transported on a litter carried by four men who were replaced at intervals. There were a few troops in uniform who provided a military escort through the streets leading to the cemetery of the church.

I had a great need to participate in this small observance for the prince. It would seem that others also had this need for I saw Gerard Gascon and Henri Pardeau. Many more people joined the procession when they saw uniforms escorting such a small coffin. Word spread quickly that it was the Dauphin, and most were saddened that he had died so young.

Perhaps to cover my own sorrow, I made an effort to speak to several citizens. For some, he was their charming Dauphin, their beautiful little prince. Some remembered him with fondness for the pleasure he had given with his little boy antics. Some even remembered his mother for her charities and Charles for his kindness to the foundlings. I would like to think that Charles, as well as his mother and father, would have been pleased at these remembrances from the people.

The procession entered the gate to the cemetery of the Church of Saint Marguerite to a prepared grave. There was no ceremony. No flowers were laid. No words, either of religion or remembrance, were spoken. The coffin was lowered into the grave and covered over in minutes. There was no marker. It struck me as somehow fitting that there was nothing to distinguish this as the grave of King Louis XVII. In death as in life, the Dauphin did not know he had been declared king.

After the procession dispersed, I stood for a time at that barren site. My throat was choked, but my thoughts became angry, and then angrier… at all of us: at the revolution and the fears it produced; at republicans who were threatened by the existence of any royals, especially one little boy; at the Committee of Public Safety and its terror; at authorities who were afraid to speak; at those of us in The Temple who should have known. Indeed, I was angry at any human with a degree of compassion, including myself, who had allowed this to happen to a child who was innocent of any wrong except that he had been born a prince.

***

My only remaining tie to the family of my King was the princess Teresa. It was another five months of uncertainty while officials waffled in their decisions regarding the Princess. At last she was released in December of 1795. Arrangements were made for her to go to Austria.

The royal family of France had been so much a part of my life, that several months later I followed the Princess, as did Gomin. We were her only two contacts with France.

#

Epilogue, The Pretenders

As told by Leroy Louis Charles.

The pretenders are actual historical characters.

There you have it. Turgy's account of what happened to the last Dauphin of France is probably as accurate as any we will ever get. How do I know this? Because I used what I considered to be a very authoritative source, de Beauchesne's biography of Louis XVII. I wanted to use Turgy to tell what happened to Charlie because he was there through everything. He did follow the royal family from Versailles, to Tuileries, to The Temple, and then later, to Austria, but I had no idea what he knew or saw. My solution was to use the information from de Beauchesne. The problem was that his book was published in 1855, long after Turgy was out of the picture or probably dead. It's a good example of why **Prisoner Prince** is historical fiction. Even though Turgy's experiences are based on reliable information, he couldn't have been quoting de Beauchesne.

The important fact is that to our best knowledge, Charlie died. That brings me to the pretenders and the same question I asked when I first learned about the Dauphin and Mr. Leroy. If Charlie died, how could Mr. Leroy claim to be him and get away with it? It was a good question. It sure kept me occupied through the years as I collected the stories of other imposters.

While the Dauphin was still in prison, rumors had already started about his escape. Soon after the announcement of the real Dauphin's death, the French police knew of seven different boys who claimed to be the Dauphin. By the time fifty years had passed, there were at least forty and maybe as many as a hundred. All the pretenders made good reading. Some of their stories had a basis in reality, some were pure fantasy, and some were just plain bizarre. Two of the best known pretenders were Jean Marie Hervagault and

John James Audubon. More about them, but first, here is a smattering about a few of the others just to give you an idea of the variety.

***

Somewhere I got a hint that a pretender tried to bring his case to the United States Congress. That means that a Congressman believed in him enough to support his cause to present it before his colleagues. I'm still trying to track that one down, but Congressional records around the 1800's weren't as comprehensive as they are now.

An entire community in Switzerland believes to this day that the dauphin made his home there on a farm.

In Prussia, two dauphins challenged each other in court. Maybe I should say three. One challenger was a pair of brothers who took turns being the dauphin.

A woman lived in the palace of Versailles for many years. She lived quietly and claimed no special attention for herself. When she died, it was discovered that she was a man, whereupon a clerk very obligingly, made a note on all the official documents that this was the body of Louis XVII. Why he would do such a thing is another mystery that I would love to solve.

Eleazer Williams was a Mohawk Indian of mixed parentage. He rejected his heritage, claimed to be the Dauphin, became an Episcopal minister and a missionary, and helped to found the town of Green Bay, Wisconsin. Nearby towns preserve that history with names like "Lost Dauphin Road," the "Lost Dauphin Park," and "Lost Louie's Restaurant." An opera by Parmentier, "The Lost Dauphin," is still performed.

There you have it. After years of detective work, the closest I could find to a prince raised by Indians was Eleazer Williams.

I learned there were tombs and gravestones with epitaphs to the Dauphin in cemeteries all over the world: Holland, Switzerland, different places in France, as well as in our own New York City and Chicago.

The more I found out about them, the more I wondered how it was that bishops, governments, senators, other important people, and entire communities accepted the pretenders on the basis of only their own words, as they did Mr. Leroy, with very little or no proof of any kind that they were who they said they were.

Mark Twain takes a poke at these princes that were appearing all over the world.. The Dauphin even found his way into *Huckleberry Finn*. As Huck and Jim traveled down the Mississippi, they met two drifters who joined them on the raft. The younger one claimed to be a duke while the old, bald-headed, gray-haired one declared he was "the late dauphin". When the duke commented that the other man looked old enough to be Charlemagne, the fake dauphin answered, *"Trouble has done it...trouble has brung these gray hairs and this premature balditude. Gentlemen, you see before you...the wanderin' exiled, trampled-on, and sufferin' rightful King of France."(38)*

The only thing that seemed to ease the sorrow of the two nobles for all they had lost, was to have gullible Huck and Jim cater to their needs while bending a knee and throwing in a "Your Grace" or "Your Majesty" as they served the two swindlers.

Jean Marie Hervagault was probably one of the most famous. In France he was known to be a vagrant, a felon, and a fraud, but people still believed him and supported his cause. Another one is John James Audubon, the American naturalist. It may not be quite fair to call him a pretender. He only hinted at being royalty and let his family make the claims for him. Right now, I'm going to try to explain how it came about that the pretenders got started in the first place. I have a couple of theories, and some good reasons, too.

First, the Dauphin's ten years of life read like a frightening fairy tale. A king and queen have their power taken from them. They and their children are put into an old castle with high towers. The king and queen are killed, and the children are left as orphans and mistreated by cruel villains. In a fairy tale, there should also be a fairy godmother who comes to rescue the children. But these children's story was real. No fairy godmother appeared. Maybe that's where all the pretenders got their start. Fairy tales are supposed to have happy endings. When real life refused to end happily, people were willing to invent happier endings.

Or maybe what was allowed to happen to the boy was so pitiful that people needed to correct history to explain the cruelty to the boy. Whatever their reasons, there were those willing to accept the stories of the Dauphin's escape, and there were those willing to accept the stories of the pretenders no matter how unrealistic.

It was the last year of the boy's life that started the controversy. Until that last year, the dauphin was imprisoned with his sister Teresa, his parents King Louis and Marie Antoinette, and the king's sister Elizabeth. While they were together, there were plenty of witnesses, and everything was recorded. There were also escapes that were planned, but for all kinds of reasons, none of them succeeded. One by one the adults were executed, and the children were left alone.

No woman in France could ascend to the throne, so the attention was focused much less on Princess Teresa. She was not the threat to the new government of the republic. Throughout the revolution, there were those who continued to support the monarchy. The young Dauphin was its living symbol. It was the boy who was the threat. It was he who was the successor to the throne and that was why he was locked up in The Tower.

As de Beauchesne described so vividly, eventually the boy was separated from his mother and put under the charge of Simon, the cobbler, and conditions for him deteriorated dramatically. Today we would say the little boy was brainwashed. He began to reject his own heritage and values and assumed the opinions of his jailers. After he was completely under their control, he was used by his keepers to testify against his mother.

During the seven months he was with Simon, he was visible to many who came to The Tower. Simon even had the boy "perform" for visitors. After Simon resigned and no one was named to replace him, that was when the boy was put into complete isolation. The guards did hear a voice answer them, but no one saw the actual boy for six months. That was when the rumors of his escape and substitution became so easy to believe.

When a doctor assigned to The Tower demanded to examine the boy, there had been more than a year of mistreatment. The execution of his father, the traumatic separation from his mother, brainwashing, isolation, and severe neglect took their toll. Up until then he had been a cheerful, friendly child. I am not surprised at all that when they broke open the locks to his cell, they found a boy who was suspicious, withdrawn, filthy and sick. The changes in the boy in that year of abuse were so dramatic that it was quite easy to believe he was not the same child.

But there were also other discrepancies. After the boy in The Tower died, an autopsy was performed on the body. No comparison can be made between the methods for autopsy done today and what was done then. But even by the standards of those days, the autopsy that was done was superficial and careless. Instead of providing answers, the autopsy contributed to more suspicions and rumors.

Scrofula and rickets were both common diseases in those days. Scrofula was a tubercular condition that often made abscesses on the body as the disease progressed. Rickets was a softening of the bones that caused limbs to deform. Both diseases took considerable time to develop.

The dauphin was examined by a doctor two years before he died. At that time it was noted that the boy had rickets and that his body was wasted and thin. There was no mention of scrofula. The autopsy report after his death on the other hand, did not mention the rickets of the previous examination. It was noted that the body was emaciated, but scrofula was listed as the primary cause of death.

There was another serious omission in the autopsy. The real Dauphin had two distinguishing features on his body: a smallpox vaccination scar on his arm, and his right ear was malformed. The autopsy report did not mention either of these identification marks. Those who wanted to believe that the Dauphin escaped, took these omissions as evidence that another boy was substituted for the Dauphin. But because the autopsy was so flawed, their argument is not as strong as it could be.

The substitution theory also had help in the way the death of the boy was handled. First there was a delay in the announcement of the death that made it seem the delay was used to hide all kinds of deceptions. But worse, Teresa, the boy's sister, and Tison, a long-time servant to the family, were both close by. Neither of them was called to identify the body. Instead, guards who had only slight contact with the boy some years before, were asked to make the identification...and that in poor lantern light. That Teresa and Tison were not called, defies good sense. It was as if they were deliberately excluded for some fraudulent reason.

The changes in the boy, the flawed autopsy, the lack of distinguishing marks, and the identification of the body by near strangers, were legitimate reasons for creating doubts about whether or not the real Dauphin had died. But something more fanciful happened that contributed to all the speculation.

Three years after the boy in The Temple was buried, there appeared a penny-dreadful novel, *The Madeleine Cemetery* (an English translation of the French title) by Regnault-Warin. Penny-dreadfuls were cheap books of fiction that could be compared to the sensationalism of tabloid magazines of today. Regnault-Warin's book certainly suited that category. The novel was a totally fictional account of the escape of the Dauphin from The Tower in a laundry basket of dirty linen. The book was published in 1798 and was widely read. As the years passed, its fiction gained greater acceptance because pretenders were using information from it as the basis for their own claims. It was the wife of Simon the cobbler who made the novel most believable. She was of sound mind in 1814 when she testified under oath that she helped the dauphin escape from The Temple in a laundry basket. She repeated this for the rest of her life and even on her deathbed.

There were numerous investigations over the years to try to

establish the truth about whether or not the dauphin had died. None of these proceedings helped. At times they even added to the confusion, as when two gravediggers who had helped prepare the actual grave, gave conflicting stories about where the body was buried. The issues became no clearer when others were asked to testify fifteen, twenty, or more years after their involvement, as was the case with Madame Simon.

Whether their purpose was for financial gain, achieving notoriety, or simply to make themselves more important, the pretenders were able to take advantage of this confusion.

One of the most notorious of all the pretenders was Jean Marie Hervagault, who was a con man *extraordinaire*. The protection, support, and acceptance he received from influential people, some royalist and some not, was remarkable. That he was able to retain this support for years was even more remarkable considering that the basis for his claims was rooted in an ever-expanding fantasy that he skillfully promoted for his own benefit.

The beginning of Jean Marie's history as a pretender has two confusing and extremely slight connections to reality. When the boy in The Temple died, Laurent was the supervisor. He had a niece, Nicole Bigot who had an illegitimate son, Jean Marie. Nicole married Hervagault who adopted the boy and gave him his name. Coincidentally, a man named Remy Bigot began to appear at The Temple during this time. No relationship between Nicole Bigot and Remy Bigot has ever been proved, but that fact was overlooked by everyone at that time.

It was enough that Laurent and Bigot had connections to The Temple. For those who wanted to, that slight coincidence made it easier to believe that Jean Marie had been substituted for the Dauphin. Jean Marie began wandering the countryside. He was arrested numerous times for vagrancy, fraud, and impersonation and was well known to the French police. After all, the government of the new republic could not allow the dauphin, even if he was a fraud, to gather supporters.

But Jean Marie did attract supporters wherever he traveled in France. Never mind that he did not in any way resemble the dauphin; that he did not have the vaccination scar or deformed ear; that he was three years older than the real prince. None of this seemed to matter to those who accepted his story, and there were many from every social level. What made Jean Marie especially believable is that he did not try to cheat or swindle. In the best tradition of great con men, he simply told his tale in such a beguiling way that people were eager to volunteer their help to him.

Although Jean Marie was already known as an imposter to local police in parts of France, he gained greater public attention in 1798 because of his experiences around the town of Chalons northeast of Paris.

The real Dauphin would have been thirteen years old at that time, most likely in ill health, and certainly not street-wise enough to support himself by living as a vagrant. Jean Marie on the other hand was healthy and seventeen years old, though he was beardless and somewhat effeminate. He was also a spendthrift, was haughty, and had a refined manner. It must have been enough for a shopkeeper in nearby Meaux. This otherwise shrewd woman of business, took Jean Marie into her home for some time and then paid for his coach fare to Chalons. In Chalons, he was taken into custody by the police who were very tolerant toward their prisoner. While he was awaiting trial, Jean Marie was allowed to wander the streets dressed as a girl. Tradespeople of the town provided clothing and food delicacies on credit. Other citizens showered him with attention and gifts. It's hard to believe that a delicate young man, on the basis that he was acting the way people assumed a prince would act, was able to seduce a whole town to believe him.

Hervagault may have remained a local pet except for a nun who visited Sister Dolorme who was the Mother Superior at the local convent. It was Sister Dolorme's habit (ha!) to often talk with Jean Marie. She believed he was the Dauphin simply because he recognized a portrait of his royal great aunt. He also told touching tales of his wanderings. She believed that he had confided his true story only to her. She wrote a letter in Jean Marie's behalf. The letter was given to the visiting nun to be delivered by hand to the Cardinal himself. In this improbable, roundabout way, eventually the princess Teresa, her uncles, most of France, and parts of Europe became aware of Jean Marie's claim to be the Dauphin.

Teresa and her uncles took the public position with Jean Marie and other pretenders, that the Dauphin had died in The Temple. On rare occasions through the years however, Teresa was known privately to look for the truth regarding her brother.

When a book about Jean Marie Hervagault was published in 1801, some information came from police records, but much of it came from Jean Marie himself. According to his own account, his father, Rene Hervagault, sold Jean Marie to be the substitute for the Dauphin in The Temple. He was able to escape in a cart of dirty linen. From his own fantasies, the book also told of his travels all over Europe; his reception in Rome by the Pope and twenty Cardinals who also marked him with a symbol on his right leg; his visits in Spain and Portugal where no less than nine rulers declared him to be the rightful king of France.

Jean Marie was jailed repeatedly by the police. At first his father came to claim him, but eventually (maybe because of the story of being sold by his father) his family disowned him altogether. He was brought to trial numerous times, but he was difficult to convict since people were reluctant to testify against him. The following example might help to explain why.

In 1806 Jean Marie inveigled his way into the infantry and had the rank of private. Yet for one entire year, this private had his own separate residence, an orderly to attend him, and he was not required to do any duty. These arrangements could never have been made without the approval of a high ranking officer. If witnesses had been willing to testify against Jean Marie, some officer would certainly have been disciplined. That could be why witnesses were less than eager to speak out against Jean Marie.

He also served for some time aboard a ship. During a naval battle, he conducted himself with honor. Then typically, following his own inner voices, he deserted. He continued his wandering, his impersonation, and his stints in jail. Finally in 1812, in jail again, he was dying. To the very end he maintained to the chaplain that he was Louis XVII. He was thirty years old when he died.

Granted, there were reasons why Jean Marie Hervagault was easily accepted by some as the dauphin, but two questions continue to be puzzling.

Why did it never become an issue that a young princeling, who was known to be ill, was roaming the countryside alone?

Why did it never become an issue that Jean Marie was still alive when, according to his own story, he was sold to be a substitute for the boy who died in The Temple?

***

The other pretender that I consider to be remarkable was John James Audubon, the naturalist. He is an altogether different personality from Hervagault. Except among his family and a few friends, John James made no attempt to draw public attention to himself as heir to the French throne. Rather, that distinction fell to Alice Jaynes Tyler, a cousin by marriage. Alice Tyler's mother-in-law Delia, was a granddaughter to John James. With this connection, Mrs. Tyler knew about Audubon family lore…that John James was adopted, that he grew up in France, and that he was born in 1785, the same year as the dauphin.

Mrs, Tyler also learned more family history when papers that were previously kept private within the Audubon family, were released to her husband, Leonard. Among these papers were a few letters that Audubon wrote to his wife Lucy. The letters were written around 1826 while he was traveling through Europe to gain support for the publication of his first book, *The Birds of America*. The letters are filled with anguish and make reference to his possible heritage as the French heir, but the references are vague and can be interpreted in different ways.

Over one hundred years later with the family stories and papers available to her, Mrs. Tyler wrote a book, *I Who Should Command All!* It was published in 1937 in honor of the opening of the Audubon Memorial Park and Museum in Henderson, Kentucky. She dedicated the book to five women of the Audubon family that she apparently idolized, and to her husband and three children who "perpetuate the line." The book is intended to establish that Audubon was the Dauphin and should have been Louis XVII, king of France.

The title of the book is a quotation from one of Audobon's letters. His letter begins with, *"I see my father before me with his proud eagle's eyes frowning on me…How I regret this journey ~ it has opened all my wounds afresh…I must try to bury the dreadful past in oblivion."* The letter ends with, *"I who should command all!"(38)* There is however, no indication in Audubon's letter as to what the "all" that he should be commanding might be.

Why Henderson, Kentucky chose to create a museum in Audubon's honor is sort of a puzzle in itself. Audubon lived in Henderson only for about ten years. It was here that his business went bankrupt, and that he barely escaped debtor's prison. In Henderson he lived as he had during the first half of his life, as a country gentleman who depended on other people to provide the means. Although he was involved with several different partners and in various business ventures in Pennsylvania, Ohio, Kentucky, Missouri, and Louisiana, his interests were in hunting, fishing, and wandering the countryside rather than tending to business. From his earliest days, he was undisciplined and directionless. His only long-term interest seemed to be in observing and sketching wildlife.

John James was born on the island of Santo Domingo (now Haiti). He was the illegitimate son of Jean Audubon who was a merchant, sea captain, slave trader, and an adventurer who traveled the world. During this period, England and France were often hostile or at war. As a consequence, Jean Audubon was captured by the English and imprisoned in New Hampshire. After his release, he became active in the American Revolution and knew both Lafayette and Washington. He also acquired property in Pennsylvania. Eventually he returned to Nantes, France. It is at this point that Mrs. Tyler makes her first argument that John James, the son of Jean Audubon, is the Dauphin.

In early 1794 rumors are already circulating that the Dauphin had disappeared from The Temple. John James is now nine years old. He and his half sister have both been cared for as the natural children of Jean Audubon. Suddenly, forty some days after Simon the cobbler leaves The Temple, Jean Audubon decides to formally adopt his two children, and Mrs. Tyler pointedly asks, "*Why should Admiral Audubon suddenly choose to legally adopt these two illegitimate children...?(39)* She proceeds to provide arguments to answer that question.

She notes that on the adoption papers, the mother of the girl is named while the name of John James' mother is not recorded. Mrs. Tyler makes the assumption that Jean Audubon is a merchant who knows the importance of proper legal papers. Why should he "*carefully omit*" the name of John James' mother?

Mrs. Tyler's contention is that the Dauphin was spirited out of The Temple, brought to Nantes, suddenly adopted by Audubon who "carefully omitted' the name of Marie Antoinette, the real mother of John James. But then, there is the problem of what happened to the boy who lived for nine years as the natural son of Jean Audubon? Mrs. Tyler suggests that perhaps that boy never existed since no name was recorded on the certificate of birth when the boy was born in Haiti.

There are a few other arguments offered by Mrs. Tyler to support her claims. Nicholas Berthoud is a continual hovering presence in the life of John James. During those periods of Audubon's financial problems, it was he who usually appeared to rescue John James. Mrs. Tyler maintains that help was provided because of the influence of Madame Berthoud, Nicholas' wife. She was believed to be a former lady-in-waiting to Marie Antoinette.

Mrs. Tyler also notes that Jean Audubon gave his adopted son attention that would be unusual to give an illegitimate son. John James himself remembered two black servants who cared for him at all times while he was a boy in Nantes. As John James approached adulthood, his father continued to take a very protective interest in him even when he was no longer required to do so. The suggestion is that perhaps the father carried a heavier responsibility for this special adopted son.

The dauphin's love of flowers and study of botany is well known, That is an easy connection to Audubon's interest in nature. But Mrs. Tyler suggests that the canaries that distracted the Dauphin from his troubles for a short time while he was in The Temple, developed into Audubon's love of birds. In contrast, it should be noted that no historians mention that the Dauphin showed any special talent for drawing or painting, while Audubon very early showed talent and interest in both.

Included in Mrs. Tyler's book are photographs not only of Audubon's outstanding work as a naturalist, but also paintings of the Dauphin and John James's two sons, Victor and John. When pictures of the Dauphin and the two boys are side by side, the resemblance is strong and hard to deny.

Though John James Audubon was not as obvious a pretender as others who were more public, he certainly helped to perpetuate the idea with his family and within his circle of friends. In one of his letters from Europe he wrote to his wife:

"We are a few miles south of the line for the second time in my life. What ideas it conveys to me of my high birth and expectations of my younger days.

My high birth, though unknown to the world, was always on my lips and I felt a pride unbecoming my situation, but I seemed to control it.

I am an aristocrat. I cannot divest myself of this knowledge; the feelings it brings remains with me. How can I help this?"(40)

Mrs. Tyler tells of one family story involving Marshall Michel

Ney, one of Napoleon's best known generals, who was believed to be living incognito in South Carolina. Ney refused to sit in Audubon's presence and was heard to say, *"He is higher than I am! He is higher than Napoleon! He is higher than anybody!"(41)*

Facts seem to create a historical problem however, since Marshall Ney was executed in France in 1815. A person might be led to suspect that one pretender was paying court to another pretender.

Granted, John James Audubon was not the most exemplary character in the first half of his life. But after the publication of his book, he received international recognition as a naturalist, ornithologist, and painter. Audubon died in 1851. His achievements were considerable. To this day Audubon Societies of bird watchers exist all over the world, not just for hobby purposes, but as a force for conservation. This is a legacy that would be more than satisfying for any family. But for the Audubon heirs and for Audubon himself, it didn't seem to be enough. For some reason they also needed the connections to royalty. Maybe an explanation for this need could be Audubon's birth.

In past centuries, illegitimacy was a disgrace not only to the individual, but to the entire family as well. Although his father accepted John James as his son, there were the years when John James was known by four different surnames. One of these names was Rabine, his mother's last name. Under French law, he was registered as Jean Rabine. When his father deeded property to him as Jean Rabine, John James refused the property and said, *"My own name I have never been permitted even to speak; accord me then, that of Audubon which I have cause to reverence."* (42)

Indeed the stigma of illegitimacy was felt even by the five granddaughters of John James to whom Mrs. Tyler's book is dedicated. Originally these ladies withheld Audubon's papers to avoid the "dreaded publicity" that would most likely result if biographers began to delve into his history. Inevitably a biographer did delve into John James's life and documented facts regarding his birth. It was in defense against this biography that the ladies, who were elderly by that time, released the Audubon letters. The letters were entrusted to Mrs. Tyler who did her best to try to establish much more desirable circumstances for the birth of John James Audubon, and so she wrote her book.

***

But it is today's science that became the determining factor in the story of the Dauphin as well as all his pretenders. Now, two hundred plus years later, after France was long established as a republic; after all the conflicting stories; after all the pretenders had lived out their lives; after the children of Louis XVI and Marie Antoinette became little more than a footnote to history and their suffering rarely mentioned, there were still a number of people who were intrigued with the mystery of what happened to the last Dauphin of France. The question was finally resolved in a clinical laboratory.

In December 1999, what was believed to be the actual heart of the Dauphin was submitted for DNA testing. How the Dauphin's heart reached a modern laboratory fits very neatly with the rest of the drama surrounding the prince. This last act which took place recently in the laboratory, actually began over two hundred years ago during the autopsy of the little boy who died in The Tower.

A doctor, Philippe-Jean Pelletan, a royalist, was present at the autopsy that was authorized and orchestrated by the government of the republic. That a royalist was present at this event is remarkable in itself. What should have been a carefully guarded, very serious, scientific procedure to establish historical accuracy, was anything but. Instead it was haphazard, bumbled, and careless, so much so that Pelletan was able to accomplish an audacious act.

Ignoring the most basic medical, ethical and moral standards, during the autopsy, Pelletan stole the heart from the body of the little boy. He hid the heart in his handkerchief, and succeeded in walking away with it. His motivation for such a bold act is unknown. It could be possible that he took the heart because he thought it might some day become important, but more likely he took it to show defiance to the republican government.

Pelletan's deed, was only the beginning. The heart changed possession many times through the years. In turn it was stolen from Pelletan by his assistant and later found its way back to the doctor. It was then given to the Archbishop of Paris for safekeeping. When the Archbishop's palace was attacked in 1830, the heart's container was smashed to pieces. Eventually the heart found its roundabout way back to Pelletan's son, and much more recently, the laboratory.

Scientists conceded that *"the heart was not ideally preserved for this test,"* (43) but tiny slivers of it were sent to laboratories in Belgium and Germany. Similar DNA tests were conducted by scientists in each country so as to better substantiate their findings. The slivers provided enough information to get results that were decisive. The DNA from the heart was traced to Marie Antoinette and her descendants. Through Pelletan's daring and unconscionable theft at that long ago autopsy, science today could prove that it was indeed the last Dauphin of France who had died in The Tower.

This may not however, be the end of the story. As might be expected and in the spirit of controversies in the past, descendants of the pretender in Switzerland are already rejecting the DNA results. That family is the first to reject the findings, but it is still early days.

***

In France, from the very beginning of the monarchy, long before the revolution, there was a principle that maintained "The king cannot die." Maybe it will be the descendants of the pretenders who will help to keep that principle alive.

***

The Last Dauphin of France, my Charlie, has been a part of

my life since I've been a boy. I've had lots of empathy for all that he endured. But besides, I liked him. In my own small way with this book, I hope to keep alive the memory of that unfortunate prince. He was forced to endure prison not as punishment for anything he did, but only because he was a prince. This is an injustice we should not forget.

The end of the book, but maybe not the end of the story.

Events in *Prisoner Prince* Presented Chronologically

Louis Auguste (King Louis XVI) born 1754

Marie Antoinette of Austria born 1755

Marie Antoinette arrived in France 1770

Louis Auguste and Marie Antoinette married 1770

Louis Auguste crowned King Louis XVI and Marie his Queen 1774

American Revolution began July 4, 1776

Axel Fersen from Sweden arrived in France 1776

Princess Teresa, first daughter to King Louis and Marie born 8-15-1777

Axel Fersen and Lafayette joined American Revolution 1778

Louis Xavier, first son to King Louis and Marie born 10-25-1781

Axel Fersen recalled to Sweden 1784

Louis Charles, second son to King Louis and Marie born 3-27-1785

Princess Sophie, second daughter to King Louis and Marie born 7-9-1786

Princess Sophie died 1787

Estates General formed, first step toward a republic in France 1788

Axel Fersen returned to Versailles early 1789

Elsa von Bradenburg from Austria arrived at Versailles May 1789

Louis Xavier, first Dauphin died 6-4-1789

Louis Charles became the Last Dauphin 6-4-1789

Estates General became the National Assembly 7-14-1789

Gerard Gaston joined the National Guard 7-30-1789

"Declaration of the Rights of Man" announced 8-20-1789

Riots at Versailles October 5 & 6, 1789

Royal Family ordered to the Tuileries 10-13-1789

Suppression of religion 2-13-1790

Abolishment of hereditary titles 6-19-1790

Civil Constitution published 7-12-1790

Disturbance around King's carriage at Easter Spring 1791

Escape from Tuileries 6-20-1791

Edict to deprive King Louis of his power. 6-21-1791

Royal Family forced to return to Tuileries 6-25-1791

First use of guillotine in a public execution April 1792

France declared war against Austria and Prussia 4-20-1792

Thousands killed in riots at Tuileries 8-12-1792

Harangues against Louis and Marie in National Assembly 8-12-1792

King Louis deposed. Family imprisoned in The Temple 8-14-1792

Princess de Lamballe murdered 9-3-1792

Massacre of prisoners September 1792

King Louis separated from his family 9-21-1792

Dauphin separated from mother and put with father 10-27-1792

King Louis trial begins. Dauphin back with mother 12-26-1792

King Louis condemned 1-17-1793

King Louis executed 1-21-1793

The Dauphin proclaimed King Louis XVII. Count Provence became Regent for the boy 1-28-1793

Dauphin taken from Mother. Simon the Cobbler became tutor 1-3-1793

Jean Paul Marat mordered by Charlotte Corday 7-13-1793

Committee of Public Safety formed with Robespierre at the head.

"Reign of Terror" began 7-27-1793

Marie Antoinette's trial began. Dauphin signs deposition 10-6-1793

Marie Antoinette executed 10-16-1793

Simon resigned as tutor to Dauphin 1-5-1794

Dauphin placed in isolation 1-20-1794

Elizabeth executed 5-10-1794

Dr.Laurent discovered Dauphin in isolation 7-27-1794

Robespierre and Simon the Cobbler executed 7-28-1794

Dauphin Louis Charles died 6-8-1795

Dauphin buried in an unmarked grave 6-10-1795

Princess Teresa released to leave for Austria December 1795

Other Interesting Dates:

Napoleon Bonaparte seized power in France 1799

Axel Fersen killed by a mob in Sweden 1810

Napoleon defeated and removed from power 1815

Count Provence restored to throne of France as Louis XVIII 1815

End Notes

1. Penny-Dreadfuls were inexpensive novels that could be compared to the tabloid newspapers of today.

2. The Society of Cincinnati was formed to help veterans of the American Revolution and their families with support and pensions. It was named after a Roman citizen, Lucius Quintus Cincinnatus, who left his farm to become a great general, and then gave up his power after his duty to the country was over.

3. The words in italics are quotations from *Louis XVII, His Life, His Suffering, and His Death* by Hyacinthe Alcide du Boise de Beauchesne published in 1855 in France. It was the major reference for *Prisoner Prince* and is cited throughout.

4. Empress Maria Theresa of Austria died in 1780. If Elsa von Bradenberg had been a real person, she could not have been writing to the Empress in 1789. The author took this liberty for purposes of the story.

5. through (13) all quotes from de Beauchesne.

6. (14) This passage is quoted from *The French Revolution* by Adrian Gilbert.

7. (15) Turgy was mentioned in historical references only by one name. He was a cook in three royal residences that are a part of this novel. I could find no other information about him. His biography and opinions were created by the author. His experiences are based on de Beauchesne's history.

8. (16) King Louis XVI did tinker with mechanisms, clocks, and

inventions. This incident with the locks in the Versailles kitchen was invented by the author to illustrate this interest as well as to establish Turgy's loyalty to the King.

9. (17) through (36) all quotes from de Beauchesne.

10. (37) Quoted from *Huckleberry Finn* by Mark Twain.

11. (38) through (42) all quotes from *I Who Should Command All!* By Alice Jaynes Tyler.

12. (43) Quoted from "The New York Times International" of December 21,1999.

Author's Note

Dear Readers,

My favorite reading genre is historical fiction. To me, this is a painless way of absorbing history. However, as I'm reading, I'm also questioning. Did that event really happen? Did he or she really take that action? Unless I already know that history, there's no way to be sure.

With that in mind, in writing my three historical novels, I've tried to keep as true as possible to actual historical characters and events. The King and Queen, Madame de Lamballe, and others are depicted very much as history recorded them.

Fictional characters like Gerard Gascon and Elsa von Bradenberg were created because I believe they help to humanize history. Gerard and Elsa both participated in actual events, but I hope their views about those events make the experiences more vivid and real.

Turgy and Axel de Fersen are special. They were both actual people, but minor characters in history. Yet they were very much involved in the lives of the royal family and in unique positions to relate what they experienced.

When fiction and history cross and there is some discrepancy, the circumstances are explained in the End Notes.

Thanks for reading. I hope you enjoy.

O. B. K.

Author's Biography

Olga B. Kurtz has had a varied career as an elementary teacher, stay-at-home mom, and as a print shop owner. During those years, writing in some form has always been important, but retirement offered the opportunity to work at this interest more seriously. The result has been three historical novels and a memoir.

Ms. Kurtz currently lives in Akron, Ohio which has been her home for most of her life, although she did live in the Buffalo, New York area for 20 years. She received her B.S. degree from Buffalo State Teachers College and also taught elementary school in West Seneca, New York.

She has two children, Christopher Kurtz and Melissa Jones, and five grandchildren. None of them live in Akron, but close enough to visit often.

Other Books By Olga B. Kurtz

Crazy Spider
(About another unfortunate prince during the Russian Revolution)

Revolución Reporter
(About the Mexican Revolution and Pancho Villa)

The Way It Was, Recollections of the Life and Times of an
Opinionated Granny

Made in the USA
Middletown, DE
23 April 2017